HIPPO **SPØRT**

THE WINNING TOUCH

David Hill

Scholastic Children's Books
Commonwealth House, 1–19 New Oxford Street,
London WC1A 1NU, UK
a division of Scholastic Ltd
London ~ New York ~ Toronto ~ Sydney ~ Auckland

First published by Ashton Scholastic NZ, 1995
First published in the UK by Scholastic Ltd, 1997

Text copyright © David Hill, 1995
Inside illustrations by Jeffrey Parker

ISBN 0 590 13643 7

Chapter 1

Zip!

Kenny Jury sent his curving, dipping, speeding up, impossible-to-hit softball pitch fizzing towards the Eastern Heights batter.

Thonk!

The Eastern Heights batter hit it. He hit it so hard that Kenny was still crouched with his arm pointing forward when the ball blurred back past.

"Catch it, Murdoch!" yelled the Welton Intermediate girls standing behind the softball diamond.

Second baseman Murdoch Boyd jumped and flung up one arm. Luckily, the gel Murdoch had put on before the game stopped his hair flopping out of place. Unluckily, the tight New York Giants T-shirt Murdoch was wearing to show off his muscles stopped his arm from reaching right up. The softball soared over his hand, bounced, and raced away across the grass.

"Stop it, Tu!" the Welton Intermediate girls yelled.

Left outfielder Tu Te Waka galloped towards the speeding softball. He reached a hand down to stop it. The ball hit a bump, bounced over Tu's hand, and raced on. Tu's foot hit the same bump. He stumbled and fell.

The Welton spectators groaned. The three Eastern Heights players who had loaded the bases jogged home easily. The Eastern Heights batter jogged around all the bases for an easy home run, and met a line-up of high fives.

"All right, boys, we'll stop there," Mr O'Neill called. "That's a win to Eastern Heights by —" Mr O'Neill mumbled the next part, "— by twenty-six to three."

The Eastern Heights team whistled and cheered and smacked one another's hands some more. Ira Esera, the Welton catcher, glared at them. They went quiet and moved away quickly.

"Welton, three cheers for Eastern Heights," called Kenny Jury, who was the Welton captain. A faint moaning noise came from the Welton team.

Ten minutes later, the Welton teams were standing by the school driveway while the Eastern Heights visiting teams climbed on board their buses.

"Hope you've got room on the bus for all the cups and shields you won this afternoon!" Mr O'Neill called, trying to sound cheerful.

4

The Eastern Heights teacher smirked. "Actually, we've still got them in the display case at school from last time," she said. "We didn't bring them with us."

Mumbles and snarls from the Welton kids.

"Be good sports," hissed Ms Benge as the bus pulled away. "Wave to them. Ira Esera! You don't wave with one finger!"

When the bus had disappeared down the drive, the Welton kids began wandering back towards their form rooms. Shayne Bradshaw was tapping away on his calculator.

"Eastern Heights won the boys' softball twenty-six to three, the girls' softball twenty-nine to four—"

"Twenty-nine to five!" Ani Niwa corrected him. "Tammy got a run in our last innings."

"Twenty-nine to five ..." Shayne made the correction on his calculator. "They won the athletics by fourteen events to two — we won't count the relay, where Dean bowled over the Eastern Heights runner ..."

"Yeah, but Dean didn't have his glasses on," Tu Te Waka explained to some of the kids who were looking puzzled. "He was in a glass of his own."

"... they won the A-team cricket and the B-team cricket and the boys' tennis," Shayne went on. "How about the girls' tennis? Does anyone know?"

"Silina Johns won her match," Tammy

5

Thompson said. "Eastern Heights won the other five."

"Pity it had to be Silina," muttered Ani. Tu and Kenny looked at each other and winked.

Shayne was totalling the results on his calculator. "Eastern Heights won all seven sports events," he announced, "with a grand total of" — Tu and Kenny put their hands over their ears — "two hundred and fifty-three points. Welton Intermediate scored a total of" — Kenny and Tu pressed their hands harder against their ears — "sixty-two points."

"We were thrashed," said Tammy.

"Massacred," Ani agreed.

"Well, it was a tricky time to play," said Ms Benge. "We're into the sign of Gemini, and anything can happen there. Am I right?"

"Right!" chorused the group gathered around Shayne, managing a few faint grins.

"Ms Benge and her stars!" sighed Kenny as they picked up their bags from the back of their form room. They sidestepped Ira, who was wandering along with Dean Gooch, glaring at anyone who came near.

"The only stars I saw were when I fell over at softball," said Tu. "Man, Kenny, we've gotta do better next time. We have to!"

"Yeah," agreed Kenny. Then he added, "How?"

Chapter 2

"Eastern Heights always thrash us," Kenny was still complaining the next morning during Room 14's roll check.

"Well, they are one of the biggest intermediate schools around," Mr O'Neill reminded him. "Ira! Sit down please, and give Jason his arm back."

"Yeah, but surely we can beat them at something," Ani groaned.

"Silina beat them at tennis," said Tu, winking at Kenny.

"Don't remind us," Tammy Thompson muttered.

Silina Johns tossed her long fair hair and said nothing. Kenny glanced at her and started to go pink. He saw Tu grinning at him, and went even pinker.

"Well, you've got winter sports starting soon," Mr O'Neill went on. "Ira! Sit down! Matiu's head does not unscrew!" He raised his voice above the usual Room 14 noise. "I'm sure you can put together a good team for some game."

"Not hockey," Dean Gooch said immediately. "The last time I played hockey my glasses got smashed. I couldn't see a thing!"

"You can't see a thing when you're *wearing* your glasses, Gooch!" jeered Murdoch Boyd. This morning Murdoch wore a T-shirt which read CHAMPION OF CHAMPIONS. A comb stuck out of the left hip pocket of his jeans. Another comb stuck out of his right hip pocket.

"Not netball," Ani Niwa said. "Eastern Heights have got all these gi-normous tall girls."

"And their girls have all got gi-normous long fingernails," Tammy added.

"How about soccer?" asked Mr O'Neill. "Ira! Put Adam down! I'm not telling you again."

"Soccer's a thinking man's game," said Shayne, looking up from his calculator.

"A thinking person's game!" Ani and Tammy snapped together. "Girls can play soccer!"

"We played Eastern Heights at soccer last year in Form One," Kenny said. "We got wasted."

"They're killers, man," Tu added. "I was black and blue and green and yellow with bruises after that game. And a bit of purple."

"Rugby?" Mr O'Neill suggested. "Right! That's enough. I'm not telling you again, Ira Esera. You're on detention tonight after school."

"Rugby!" Tu repeated, shaking his head in

amazement. "Have you seen the size of those guys, Mr O'Neill? They make King Kong look underfed."

"I don't mean ordinary rugby," said their teacher. "I mean New Image rugby."

At the words "New Image", Silina looked interested. So did Murdoch, who took out his left comb and ran it through his hair.

"New Image? Sounds like a shampoo or something," Dean said. Silina and Murdoch looked even more interested. "I've never seen New Image rugby."

"*You've* never seen —" Murdoch began, then stopped when he realised Ira was turning towards him. Big, beefy Ira and small, short-sighted Dean hung around together, "a bit like a Rottweiler and a chihuahua," as Tu had described them once — when Ira wasn't there.

"New Image rugby is the sort where you don't tackle people, you just tag them," Mr O'Neill explained. "So it doesn't really matter what size you are. You still have scrums and lineouts, but there's no pushing or shoving. The game's been designed specially for schoolkids."

"How many in a team?" Kenny wanted to know. Room 14 was getting less noisy as more kids started to listen. Mr O'Neill, who wasn't used to a quiet class, hesitated, then hurried on.

9

"You can have ten or twelve," he said. "It's up to the team, really."

Shayne's fingers flickered over his calculator keys. "Ten in a team would mean fifty percent more room on the field for each player," he announced. Silina rolled her eyes.

"Yes, it's a really fast game," Mr O'Neill added. "Lots of passing and running." He paused for a moment. "If any of you boys are interested" — this time Ani and Tammy rolled their eyes — "come to Top Field after school. We'll see what you think."

"You're home late, son," said Mr Jury when Kenny walked in through the back door. "Have you and Tu been delivering circulars?"

"Nah, that's Thursdays. We had a sort of a practice to see if any of the guys wanted to try playing this New Image rugby."

"Any good?" his father asked.

Kenny shrugged. "The game's pretty cool, but only eleven guys turned up, and a lot of them only wanted to muck about. Ira Esera just came to get out of detention. He kept running into people on purpose — big thug."

"Tu there?"

"Yeah, Tu, and Murdoch Boyd — Murdoch's good, but not as good as he thinks he is — and

Shayne and his calculator, and Dean and his glasses. Plus that guy Dallas Orr — that really shy guy from Ms Benge's class."

"Yes, I know Dallas," Mr Jury said. "His fa—" He stopped suddenly.

"The others were just a pack of idiots," Kenny grumbled, "kicking the ball into the macrocarpas and that. They wouldn't take any notice of Mr O'Neill. What time's dinner, Dad?"

"I'm just going to start the vegetables now," his father replied. "Your mum should be home about five-thirty. Feel like boiled cabbage?"

"Boiled cabbage!" groaned Kenny. "Gross."

"Just as well I'm not cooking any then," his father grinned. "So — New Image rugby is not the right image for Welton Intermediate, eh?"

"Well, Mr O'Neill is going to ask in assembly tomorrow if anyone wants to join. He hasn't got a hope, I reckon ..."

Chapter 3

"I told Ms Benge about last night's practice," Tu told Kenny as they joined the crowd pushing into the assembly hall next morning. "She said it's always difficult when the new moon rides above the sun, or something. Sounds like a western, eh?"

Kenny said nothing. He'd just spotted Silina Johns. Now he was aiming for the row behind her, while trying to make it look as though he wasn't. Tu grinned and followed him.

"Did you see Ms Benge talking to Mr O'Neill while the teachers were leaving assembly?" Shayne Bradshaw wanted to know as they made their way to class.

"Maybe she was putting stars in his eyes?" smirked Murdoch.

As they entered the uproar of Room 14, Kenny whispered to Tu, "I know — I'll ask Ms Benge how to send Murdoch into orbit."

A breeze was stirring the macrocarpa trees at one end of Top Field as Tu and Kenny and Shayne headed up the steps after school. Shayne had his calculator out and was murmuring something about the height-width ratio of each step.

When they reached the field, the three boys found Ani Niwa and Tammy Thompson sitting on the grass picking daisies and threading them into a chain.

"We're gonna be using this field for New Image rugby," Kenny told them.

"We know," Tammy and Ani replied together.

"Come to watch some classy guys in action, have you?" asked Tu. Murdoch Boyd, coming up the steps behind them, saw the two girls and quickly checked his hair.

Ani poked out her tongue at Tu. "Hardly any guys here at all," she said, "let alone classy ones."

"Here come two more," Shayne announced, as Dean Gooch's glasses came glinting up the steps with Ira Esera's shoulders looming beside them. "That increases the number by fifty percent."

Kenny looked at Ira, then raised his eyebrows at Tu.

"Mr O'Neill gave him another detention this morning," whispered Tu.

Kenny began to smile, then stopped and swallowed. Silina Johns had appeared at the top of the steps. She sat down a little distance away from Tammy and Ani and pushed her hair back behind her ears. Murdoch reached for his comb again.

"Hi, Dallas," called Tu as another figure emerged from the steps. The newcomer nodded shyly.

"Dallas makes seven," said Shayne. "That's seventy percent of a team."

"That's not many," Dean said. Ira grunted. Kenny thought about saying that Ira made up for two people, but decided against it.

"Here's Mr O'Neill," announced Tu. "Hey — and Ms Benge. She must've come to meet the stars, eh?"

Mr O'Neill saw all the Form Two eyes staring at him and Ms Benge. He looked embarrassed. "Right. Who've we got?" he asked quickly.

"Not many," Kenny told him. "Only seven."

And then Ms Benge made the Welton Intermediate boys see stars after all. "More than that," she said, looking around. "I make it ten."

Kenny and Tu and Shayne and Murdoch and Dean and Ira and Dallas all stared at the two teachers for a second. Then they looked at Ani and Tammy and Silina sitting on the grass. Dallas said nothing. Ira rumbled. The others all spoke at once. "Girls?"

"So?" said Ms Benge. "Why not girls?"

14

"Yeah, why not girls?" Ani asked as she and Tammy stood up.

"We can play New Image if we want to," Silina added, unfolding her long legs and standing up also.

"Yeah, that's right!" Ani and Tammy said together. Then they looked at each other in surprise.

"Ten gives you exactly enough for a team, doesn't it?" asked Ms Benge. "In fact ... looks like you're going to have a reserve as well."

Another figure stood at the top of the steps, chewing on a large chunk of gum. A very small figure with brown hair shaved above the ears, and spiky bits sticking up on top. A figure with three silver studs in each ear.

"It's that bikie kid from Form One!" Murdoch hissed.

"She used to play with my little sister!" Tu gasped.

"This is Holly Potroz," said Ms Benge. "When I told the girls in my PE class about New Image rugby, Holly was really interested."

The ten Form Two kids stood and stared. Mr O'Neill cleared his throat. "All right, everybody. We've got enough for a team, so let's get organised."

"A rugby team with four girls in it!" Dean

15

muttered. "The other schools are gonna waste us."

"A rugby team with a Form One bikie girl in it!" Tu shook his head. "The other schools are gonna rubbish us!"

Chapter 4

"New Image rugby still going, I see?" Mr Jury looked up from folding the washing as Kenny limped painfully inside later that Wednesday afternoon.

"Yeah, sort of."

"Good practice was it?"

"Yeah, sort of."

"Hard one, too, by the looks of it." Mr Jury watched his son hobble across the room.

"Yeah, sort of."

Kenny tossed his schoolbag into his room, limped into the living room, and turned on the television.

He didn't really see the characters in the cartoon. His mind was busily replaying pictures of the practice just finished. So many pictures that Kenny almost needed Shayne's calculator to count them.

He remembered how they'd learned the New Image way of tackling — a tag with two hands on the opponent's hips. The first time Murdoch did it to Silina, she whirled around, smacked him on the side of the head and yelled, "Keep your grubby hands to yourself, Murdoch Boyd!"

Ani and Tammy burst out laughing. Murdoch's mouth fell open, then he began combing his hair where Silina had hit him.

"It's all right, Silina," Ms Benge called out. "It's all part of the game. The bottom line is that your bottom's still okay. Right?"

"Right!" chorused the others — except Murdoch and Silina.

"Better not tag Murdoch on the bum," Kenny whispered to Tu. "His brains might get bruised."

Kenny also remembered Dean accidentally colliding with people as he raced around without his glasses; Ira deliberately colliding with people until Ani and Tammy rammed him at the same time from both sides; Shayne announcing that 57.5 percent of all passes had been dropped; Dallas, catching and dodging and tagging and passing (until Tammy said, "Hey, Dallas! You're good!" then ducking his head shyly and not doing much at all for the next five minutes); Silina flashing by, her long legs chasing Tu across the field; Tu flicking a pass behind him, Ani catching it and dodging downfield until Dallas tagged her; Ira taking Ani's pass and pretending to go one way then turning the other, roaring "Here, mate!" and slinging the ball halfway across the field to Dean, who somehow caught it and sprinted over the goal line while everyone else looked at one another and grinned.

"Well, well," said Mr O'Neill.

"You must be an Aquarian, Dean, are you?" called out Ms Benge.

"No, Ms Benge, I'm a Gooch," Dean replied. Everyone's grins grew wider.

But most of all, Kenny remembered Holly Potroz; the small figure with spiky hair, chasing and tagging everyone she could catch, including some on her own side.

Almost at the end of practice, Dallas got the ball and flicked it to Kenny. The only person for Kenny to beat was Holly. As she raced to tag him, Kenny stuck out his hand to push her away.

Just as Mr O'Neill started to call "No fen—", Kenny remembered you weren't allowed to fend in New Image rugby, and pulled his hand back. Rather, he tried to pull his hand back. Quick as a blink, Holly grabbed his wrist with both hands and yanked him forwards. One of her small feet shot out and hooked behind Kenny's ankle. The other foot kicked him hard on the side of the knee. Kenny crumpled in a heap and the ball bounced away across the grass.

Total silence. Mr O'Neill looked as if he'd swallowed his whistle.

Holly ran a hand through her spiky hair. She shifted her gum to the side of her mouth. "I didn't mean to, sorry," she said to Kenny, "but that's what they teach us at karate."

Chapter 5

Practice after school the next day, Thursday, was to be a short one. Tammy had a piano lesson at four o'clock. Tu and Kenny had to deliver circulars.

Practice turned out to be even shorter than expected. Thursday was not a good day for the Welton Intermediate School New Image rugby team. ("We've got to find a better name than that!" said Shayne.)

First, Kenny had to put up with the other kids' jokes about how Holly Potroz — the battling baby bikie, Tu called her — had bowled him at practice the day before.

"A couple of my brothers reckon everyone's scared to practise with her at karate," said Ani, which made Kenny feel a bit better.

"I'll get my little sister to give you some tips on self defence," said Tu, which didn't make Kenny feel a bit better.

Then, in a Room 14 that was even noisier than

usual, Murdoch got only one of his eight Maths sets correct.

"You can't rely on good looks to carry you through life, Murdoch," Mr O'Neill told him. Murdoch sulked.

Meanwhile, Silina had actually got one of her eight Maths sets wrong. Since Silina was usually top in everything, this was enough to make some of the kids mutter things she was meant to hear.

"Never mind, Silina," Mr O'Neill joked. "You can't be right all the time." Silina also sulked.

Even Mr O'Neill was having a bad day.

"Every time he opens his mouth he puts both feet in it," Tu whispered to Kenny.

"We'll see you at practice tonight, okay Ira?" Mr O'Neill asked.

Ira did what he usually did when a teacher spoke to him. He looked at the floor and said nothing.

Mr O'Neill tried to lighten things up with a joke. "Well?" he said. "You can come even when you haven't got detention, you know, Ira."

There were a few sniggers from other parts of the class. Ira kept looking at the floor.

Mr O'Neill started to get annoyed. "Other people are relying on you, Ira. You can't just think of yourself all the time when you're part of a team, you know."

"Mr O'Neill —" Dean began. The teacher's hand flicked at Dean to be silent.

"Anyway," Mr O'Neill went on, "the training'll be good for you. Help you get fitter. Lose a bit of weight, eh?" The moment he'd spoken, Mr O'Neill looked as if he wanted to bite off his own tongue.

The sniggers stopped. Ira lifted his head and stared at the teacher, then looked down again. "I'm not coming," he mumbled.

"Pardon?" demanded Mr O'Neill, his neck turning red. "Speak up, please."

"Not coming," Ira mumbled again.

The red on Mr O'Neill's neck spread to his face. "I'll expect you on Top Field for practice tonight, Ira Esera," he said. "It's time you started showing a bit of loyalty to other people. And please have the good manners to look at me when I'm talking to you."

Ira's head stayed down. Mr O'Neill stood still for a few seconds. Then he strode over to the blackboard and started scribbling notes on it.

For the next half-hour, Room 14 was quieter than it had been all year.

"Mr O'Neill shouldn't have said that to Ira," Ani muttered when they went outside at interval.

"He knows that," Shayne said. "Didn't you see the look on his face?"

"We've gotta have Ira in the team," Kenny said. "We need somebody to scare the opposition."

"How about Holly Potroz?" suggested Tu, looking innocent.

"Very funny. Forgive me if I forget to laugh," snapped Kenny.

"Somebody should tell Ira that Mr O'Neill was wrong," suggested Tammy.

"You do it, Tammy," said Shayne, as Ira bulldozed through the door of the classroom block, shouldering other kids aside.

"Not just now, thanks," replied Tammy. "I'm not insured."

Ira wasn't at practice after school. Neither was Dallas Orr.

"Anybody know where Dallas is?" Mr O'Neill wanted to know. He didn't ask about Ira.

The others shook their heads. Nobody seemed to know much about Dallas.

"He's weird," Silina announced.

"He's a loner," said Tu. "The Lone Dallas."

"With him and Ira away, we're missing nineteen-point-eight percent of our playing strength," Shayne reported. Mr O'Neill pretended not to hear.

24

The remaining 80.2 percent didn't have much of a practice. Silina was still sulking, and every time she was tagged she just threw the ball over her shoulder without trying to pass properly. A big kick-off by Murdoch hit one of the macrocarpa trees and bounced down the far bank into a drain.

"I'm not going in there!" Murdoch protested. "There's eels in there!"

"Aw, diddums!" jeered the girls, while the boys pretended to be busy with other things.

Ani and Tammy weren't speaking to Mr O'Neill because of what he'd said to Ira, and Dean didn't seem very interested without his friend. Kenny was still limping slightly from Wednesday's practice. Only Tu and Shayne seemed keen — and Holly Potroz, who was proving to be almost as good at dodging as Dallas, and who never stopped chewing her gum.

The practice ended when Tammy announced she had to go to her piano lesson. The others trailed down the steps.

"Aw well," said Tu, "if we don't have a team, at least Eastern Heights can't thrash us."

Nobody laughed.

When Kenny got home that evening, after he and Tu had delivered 300 SUPA-SHOPPA! SUPA-SAVE!

SUPA-SPECIAL! circulars into letterboxes that were often too small to take them, his father started to ask, "Hi, mate. How was —"

When he saw the expression on his son's face, he just carried on cutting the next day's lunches.

Chapter 6

"Saw Ms Benge talking to Mr O'Neill this morning," Tu greeted Kenny on Friday.

"She must be the only one who is," Kenny grunted.

Each Friday, Welton Intermediate's Form Two spent most of the morning up the road at Welton High School, doing Workshop Skills. This week, Kenny's group were starting Woodwork.

"Whatcha going to make?" Tu wanted to know.

"Think I'll make a wooden spoon," Kenny replied. "That's what they give to the bottom team, don't they?"

Dallas Orr was parking his old bike in the bike-racks when Kenny, Tu and Shayne reached the High School.

"Hey, Dallas!" Tu called. "Why weren't you at practice last night?"

Dallas ducked his head. "My dad needed me home yesterday," he murmured, and went quickly up the steps into the Woodwork room. The other three looked at each other, and six eyebrows lifted.

The Form Two's were back at their own school just before lunchtime. They'd enjoyed Woodwork. Kenny had decided to make a wooden tea-towel holder instead of a wooden spoon. Murdoch was working on a wooden handle for a hairbrush. ("Of course," grinned Tu.) Silina was making a wooden frame for a mirror, and was already well ahead of the others. ("Naturally," grinned Tu.) Ani and Tammy were working together on a stool. ("It's not easy," warned the Woodwork teacher. "Girls can do anything!" Ani and Tammy told him.)

When they arrived in Room 14, there was a message on the board in Mr O'Neill's handwriting: *New Image Rugby Team Meeting — start of lunchtime. IMPORTANT!*

"Do we have a team to have a meeting?" Kenny wondered aloud.

"We'll soon find out," said Shayne as the bell went for lunch.

He and Kenny and Tu sat down. Ani and Tammy did the same. Murdoch came in, checking his reflection in the window. Silina followed and sat next to Murdoch. Kenny looked glum. Dallas entered and sat by himself. Holly came in carrying a pink schoolbag with HEAVY METAL RULZ written

28

on it in silver marker pen. She said "Hi" and sat down, chewing gum and swinging legs that were too short to touch the ground.

Then four people entered together: Dean and Ira through the outside door, Mr O'Neill and Ms Benge through the corridor door. Ira didn't look at Mr O'Neill. Mr O'Neill didn't look at Ira.

Mr O'Neill gave an embarrassed-sounding cough and started speaking. "We've got all eleven of you? That's great."

"Eleven is a good zodiac number for times of peace," Ms Benge said, and winked at the kids. "Am I right?"

Mr O'Neill broke in before anyone had a chance to answer. "There's something I want to say to one of you, and I want the whole team to hear it. Ira—"

Oh no, thought Kenny, and he sensed the others go still. Please Mr O'Neill, not again.

"Ira," Mr O'Neill continued, "I want to apologise for what I said to you yesterday in class. I was right out of order. No teacher should ever speak to a pupil like that, and I'm very sorry."

Every face turned to Ira. He sat with his elbows on his knees, his chin in his hands, and his eyes on the floor. He didn't look up, but mumbled, "No problem."

"And I hope—" Mr O'Neill went on as the faces all turned towards him, "that you'll still be in the

New Image team, where we all want you."

All faces swivelled towards Ira. Again, he mumbled, "No problem."

"Thanks, Ira," Mr O'Neill said, looking as if he felt ten kilos lighter. "Now, we need to sort out a few things ... like, who's going to play where."

"Tammy and I want to go together," said Ani immediately.

"A Pisces and an Aquarius." Ms Benge smiled. "You two could rule the world!"

"Er ... yes," agreed Mr O'Neill. "Okay then, Ani and Tammy can be forwards. We need three people for a scrum, so you can be the two props. Now — a hooker to go in the middle. Tu?"

"No way, Mr O'Neill!" Tu shook his head. "I'm not letting those two girls grab me. They pinch!"

"Chicken!" Tammy and Ani jeered.

Mr O'Neill scratched his nose. "Well ... we need someone who can hook the ball back quickly. Someone not too tall. We need—"

"Me," announced Holly.

Everyone looked at the tiny figure with its glitter of earstuds. Ani and Tammy stood up.

"Yeah, come on Holly," Ani said. "Let's show these guys how it's done."

Ani and Tammy stood on each side of Holly. They put their arms around one another's waists and bent over, scrum-style.

"Let's try it, Mr O'Neill," Tammy urged.

Looking slightly dazed, Mr O'Neill produced a rugby ball from a cupboard. "Shayne — you, Tu and Kenny be the opposing forwards."

"But I might cut myself on Holly's hair!" Tu protested.

When the two front rows locked together, Mr O'Neill rolled the ball in between them. There was a flicker of movement, then—

"Hey! Where's the ball?" Tu asked.

"Too late," replied Silina. "Holly's already hooked it back!"

The girls stood up. Holly was grinning and chewing at the same time.

"Told you," said Ani. "Girls can do anything!"

Mr O'Neill smiled. "Now, the other position we must work out is fullback. We need someone who's good at judging distances and deciding angles and positions and—"

"Shayne!" came a chorus of voices. Mr O'Neill smiled some more.

"Hey!" said Dean, who was polishing his glasses and addressing nobody in particular. "We're gonna be the Welton All Blacks ..."

"Yeah, well don't start spitting on the ground like they do," said Shayne. "You gotta conserve your body moisture."

"We do need a proper name though," Dean

went on, replacing his glasses and looking at people this time.

"You do," nodded Ms Benge. "I wonder ..."

"That's it!" interrupted Murdoch. "The Wonderers! We can be the Welton Wonderers."

"You mean Wanderers, thickhead!" Tu laughed. Murdoch looked embarrassed.

"I think Wonderers is a cool name," Silina said suddenly. "It's different. We can play wonderfully — and we can keep the other teams wondering."

Mr O'Neill and Ms Benge grinned. "So now you're the Welton Wonderers New Image Rugby Team," said Ms Benge. "Am I right?"

"Right!" chorused nine voices. Dallas simply nodded, and Ira gave a rumble of approval.

"The Welton Wonderers," Tu repeated to Kenny as they biked home that afternoon. "Like it?"

"It's okay I s'pose," grumbled Kenny. He was wishing that Murdoch hadn't been the one who suggested it, and that Silina hadn't supported him quite so quickly.

32

Chapter 7

"Yoo-hoo! Kenny!" Mrs Jury called on Sunday morning. "Phone! It's Tu."

"Yoo-hoo to you," said Tu, when Kenny answered the phone.

"Yoo-hoo to you, too, Tu," said Kenny right back.

"Hey, that stuff Ms Benge was telling us at the end of Friday's meeting — you know, after we'd decided our team name — what'd she mean by 'train, don't sprain'?"

"Train, don't strain," Kenny laughed. "She meant get fit, but don't stuff yourself in the process."

"Oh, right. Hey, shall I come over to your place and we'll go for a training run?"

"Yeah, okay ..." Kenny began. Then, "No, tell you what, I'll come over to your place and we'll go for a run from there."

"That wouldn't be because you have to go past Silina Johns' house on the way, would it?" Tu asked.

"Dunno what you're talking about," grunted Kenny. "See ya soon."

Kenny didn't see Silina on the way to Tu's place. But as he and Tu puffed along on their training run they did see Tammy Thompson and Ani Niwa puffing along in the opposite direction.

"You guys are so slow!" called Ani.

The two boys starting sprinting — till they were around the next corner.

Around the corner after that they met Holly Potroz, on her way to karate.

"Hi," said Holly, and blew a bubble of gum.

"It's all right, Kenny," Tu panted. "I'll protect you."

"I didn't know they made karate outfits that small," Kenny panted back when Holly was out of sight.

"We've got a game on Wednesday," Mr O'Neill said casually on Monday afternoon, when everyone was up on Top Field.

"A game!" gasped nine voices, while Ira and Dallas stared.

"St Jude's are starting a New Image rugby team too," explained Ms Benge. "They'd like a practice game. Mr O'Neill told them you lot would treat them gently."

"I've got a cousin at St Jude's," said Tu. "I bet he's in the team. Choice! I'll murder him!"

Their first game only two days away! Everyone trained hard. And they found they still had a lot to learn.

"Dead ball!" Mr O'Neill called after an accidental little flick from Ira's hand had sent it halfway down the field and over the goal line.

"Dead ball?" repeated Ani. "I didn't know it had been alive!"

"You can jump and tap the ball back with your inside arm," Mr O'Neill explained later to the three forwards, Ani, Tammy and Holly, while he showed them how to stand in the lineouts.

Holly looked up at him, the sun glinting off her ear studs. "But both my arms are on the outside!" she protested.

To finish the practice, Mr O'Neill made everyone call for passes, so that the runner with the ball knew where to throw it.

The field rang with voices, yelling "Shayne!" "Murdoch!" "Kenny!" "Tammy!" Even Dallas and Ira made murmuring or rumbling noises.

Tu called "Shorty! Here, Shorty!" when Holly had the ball, but it quickly changed to "Holly!" when a small spiky head turned and glared at him.

Silina called "I'm here, Kenny! I'm here!" and

35

Kenny ran straight into Dean, who was having his usual problems without his glasses.

For the next two days, everyone felt anxious about the game against St Jude's. With nine of the nervous team members in Mr O'Neill's class, Room 14 was strangely quiet. Mr O'Neill looked as if he thought New Image rugby was a wonderful idea.

"My mum's not too keen on me playing rugby," Shayne said at lunchtime on Tuesday. "She calls it 'thugby'."

"Dad likes me playing," Ani grinned. "He says it might tire me out, and stop me hassling him and my brothers at home. Poor feeble males."

When the three o'clock bell rang on Wednesday, ten Form Twos and one Form One got changed and made their way up the steps to Top Field.

Holly Potroz was wearing black trackpants with a packet of gum sticking out of one pocket. Murdoch had black shorts with red lightning flashes on them, and a comb sticking out of one pocket. Dean wore long, baggy, green-and-orange-and-pink shorts that just showed his knees. Silina had short blue ones that showed lots and lots of her long legs. Kenny tried not to look too much.

"Hey, Dallas, did you get that at practice?" asked

Tammy, pointing to a bruise turning yellow on Dallas Orr's left thigh.

"No," mumbled Dallas.

Mr O'Neill looked as if he was going to say something to Dallas, but didn't. Instead he nodded towards Ms Benge, who was busy reading Shayne's stars: "Don't get too wrapped up in facts and figures today. And if you do, don't blame it on your horoscope!"

"Ms Benge is going to be my helper — your co-coach," announced Mr O'Neill, looking awkward.

"Didn't know you stammered, Mr O'Neill," grinned Tammy.

Everyone fell silent as a dozen or so unfamiliar figures appeared at the top of the steps.

"Hey! They've got girls!" whispered Ani.

"Hey! They've got jerseys!" Murdoch hissed.

Sure enough, the St Jude's team were all wearing light blue rugby jerseys.

"We'll talk about a uniform next practice," Ms Benge said quickly.

The two teams looked at each other. Murdoch stared jealously at the St Jude's rugby jerseys. The St Jude's players stared nervously at the size of Ira Esera, and disbelievingly at the size of Holly Potroz.

"Hi, cuz!" Tu yelled. He waved at a boy in a light blue jersey, who grinned and waved back.

"Dean, you can be reserve for the first half," said Mr O'Neill. Ira looked alarmed.

The two teams lined up. The St Jude's coach, who was refereeing the first half, blew his whistle. A St Jude's player gave the ball an almighty boot and the game was on.

Chapter 8

For the first few minutes, the Welton Wonderers were too nervous to do anything other than chase and run and tag. The thudding of sneakers on the ground, the slapping of hands on the ball, the puffing of lungs on the players, and the occasional blast on the referee's whistle were the only noises on the field.

Then Tammy took the ball in a lineout.

"Call! Call!" shouted Ms Benge.

"Tammy!" yelled Shayne, and Tammy flicked him the ball. Shayne made a lightning calculation of angles, positions and distances, and raced across the field.

"Shayne!" called Kenny. Shayne whipped a pass to him. Kenny dodged a St Jude's player then passed to Ani who ran one way, then another.

"Ani!" came Murdoch's call. Ani tossed a long pass to Murdoch, who swerved outside a diving St Jude's player, tore across the goal line, and thumped the ball down on the ground. The

Welton players jumped and yelled and cheered.

The St Jude's kids were nervous, too. Every time Ira came near one of them, they passed the ball. The first time one of them ran towards Holly, she dropped into a karate stance with her fists up. After that, St Jude's passed the ball whenever they came near Holly, too.

But St Jude's had good players. One of them scooped up a bad pass from Silina, dodged inside Dallas and scored. "Good on ya, cuz!" cheered Tu, then looked embarrassed when he remembered they were on different sides.

Holly hooked the ball from a scrum near the St Jude's line, and Kenny was across to score before anyone could touch him. Ira roared downfield with the ball in one hand, passed to Silina outside him who quickly passed it back again, and Ira thundered across the goal line while Dean danced on the sideline.

Then the Welton Wonderers dropped a pass. A St Jude's girl rushed through, picked it up as Welton turned to chase, and skimmed away for a try.

Murdoch threw the ball into a lineout; the ball landed on Holly's spiky head and bounced back over the sideline. Everyone laughed and the whistle blew for half time.

"You're winning, three–two!" exclaimed Ms Benge.

"It's fifteen–ten, actually," Mr O'Neill corrected her. "You get five points for a try."

"Shouldn't we be having kicks at goal?" Shayne wanted to know.

"We'll do that when the competition proper starts," said Mr O'Neill. "Tu Te Waka — is that a can of Coke you're drinking?"

Tu looked surprised. "Yeah. I'm thirsty. Want some?"

The second half began with Mr O'Neill as referee. Dean came on to replace Dallas, and Ira looked pleased. Dean was still squinting around, trying to work out who was where, when a St Jude's player raced past him and scored.

Murdoch got the ball from the kick-off. Tu began to call for it. "Mur-*burrrpp*!" The half-time Coke was giving him problems. Murdoch looked startled and dropped the ball. St Jude's grabbed it, flicked three quick passes, and scored again.

For the next five minutes, nobody scored. Both teams were chasing and tagging as much as they could. "Oww!" yelped a St Jude's boy after Holly Potroz tagged him hard on the hips. He spent the next few minutes rubbing his bottom.

Then the ball came to Ira. As two St Jude's players went to tag him, Ira bellowed "Dean!" and flung a huge pass right across the field.

The ball landed in Dean's hands. He peered around.

"Left!" boomed Ira. Dean took off to the left, beating a St Jude's player. "Right!" boomed Ira. Dead dodged right, beating another player. "Straight!" boomed Ira. Dean tore straight ahead and scored beside the posts. The whistle blew for full time.

"Twenty points each," announced Mr O'Neill. "Well done, both teams."

"Welton Wonderers, three cheers for St Jude's!" called Tammy. "Hoop-ray! Hoop-ray! Hoop-ray"

Ira grinned at Dean. Silina smiled at Kenny. Ms Benge smiled at everybody. "Your planets must be in good orbits," she said. "Am I right?"

"Right!" they all cheered.

"Just one thing, Ms Benge," added Murdoch. "What do the planets say about our chances of getting some decent rugby jerseys?"

"My cuz in the St Jude's team says Eastern Heights are starting a New Image team," Tu told the other Welton Wonderers at practice the next afternoon.

"Aw no!" groaned Ani and Tammy.

"And they've got Jay Viliamu and Troy McCracken in it — those two really fast guys from the softball team that trashed us."

"Aw no!" groaned Kenny and Shayne.

Chapter 9

The Thursday practice was a short one, like the previous week's had been. Tu and Kenny had to deliver advertising circulars (BE THE FIRST IN YOUR STREET WITH A FABULOUS GARDEN GNOME KITCHEN TIDY. JUST STEP ON THE PEDAL AND UP POPS HIS HEAD!). Tammy had a piano lesson — "and Dad says I'm not to miss it just because of rugby."

They had what Mr O'Neill called a 'soft' practice, since they were still feeling creaky from the game against St Jude's.

"We'll need a place-kicker to convert our tries," he said. "Murdoch, you're a pretty good kicker. Want to give it a go? All conversions are taken from right in front of the posts in New Image rugby."

Murdoch placed the ball on the ground in front of the goal posts. He stepped back and smoothed his hair, while Tu and Kenny whispered to each other, "Hope he misses. Hope he misses." He stepped forward and kicked the ball between the posts and into the macrocarpa trees.

"Just kick it over the crossbar, Murdoch — not over the horizon!" called Ms Benge, while the team searched in the trees and argued over who should look in the drain.

Practice finished with a game. When Mr O'Neill put Ira and Dean in different teams, Ira grumbled and growled and went around shoulder-charging people till the coach changed his mind.

The game finished with Ira getting a pass from Dean. Instantly, Holly zipped across from the opposite team, reached up, snatched the ball from Ira's hands and started to run towards the goal line.

Mr O'Neill blasted his whistle. "You can't do that, Holly! You can't just snatch the ball off the other team! That's a penalty against you."

"Okay," said Holly, chewing away. Ignoring the others who were all giggling nervously, she trotted back across to Ira and handed him the ball. "Here y'are."

Ira looked down at Holly, looked at the ball, and back at Holly again. A slow grin moved across his face. "Nice one," he rumbled.

"Hey, Mr O'Neill," asked Silina as they descended the steps from the field, "how about our team jerseys?"

44

"Ah, yes, well ... I haven't had much luck with that as yet. But Ms Benge has a friend who can probably get us some hockey shirts."

"Hockey shirts!" chorused Shayne, Tu, Kenny and Tammy.

"Gross!" grumbled Murdoch.

"Well, at least they should fit you," Ms Benge said. "Most of you, anyway," she added, glancing at Ira.

"We need a team mascot," Kenny said to Tu as they delivered circulars. "All sports teams have mascots."

"We could use Holly Potroz," Tu suggested. "She's small enough. Or ... I know, what about that teddy bear you keep hidden in your wardrobe?"

Kenny said nothing more about a mascot.

"First competition game tomorrow morning," announced Mr O'Neill at Friday's team meeting. "We're playing Stratton Road —"

"Mr O'Neill —" began Tammy.

"Stratton Road?" echoed Tu. "Hey, I've got a cousin there, too."

"Mr O'Neill —" Tammy tried again.

"Just a second, Tammy — at Jubilee Park, ten o'clock. So I'd like you all to be there by nine-thirty, please."

"Mr O'Neill," Tammy said a third time. "My dad doesn't want me to play."

Mr O'Neill stopped. "Why not?" he asked.

"He reckons rugby's no game for girls. I told him it's not really rugby, and not to be so sexist, but he still doesn't want me to play."

"My mum's not too keen about me playing, either, actually," Shayne chipped in. "She still calls it thugby."

"They just don't know what New Image is like," Tammy added.

"If Tammy's not playing, then I'm not either," said Ani.

"Be a pity to split up two signs that work so well together," murmured the co-coach.

Mr O'Neill was silent for a moment. "Look, Tammy and Shayne," he suggested, "why don't you two ask your parents to come along and watch tomorrow's game? Let them see that it's a game for everyone."

"Hey!" said Dean. "Why don't we all ask our parents to come and watch? Get a parent supporters group going?"

There was a chatter of approval.

"Most parents need support," Tu agreed.

"Oh, and one other thing," said Ms Benge as the meeting ended. "My friend has arranged those hockey shirts for us to have tomorrow."

Chapter 10

"Is Mum coming?" Kenny asked before he and his father left for Jubilee Park the next morning.

"Sorry, matey, she has to work. Every dollar helps, these days."

They picked up Tu on the way to Jubilee Park. Tu's Dad was working, and his mum had already promised to watch Tu's little sister playing netball.

As they parked the car at the sports ground, two figures walked past. "Morning Folau. Morning Tom," said Mr Jury as he got out and locked the car.

The large, dark figure rumbled a reply. The smaller man with the thick glasses peered in the direction of the voice and said, "Hello? Oh, that you, Karl? Great day, isn't it?" He flung out an arm, almost whacking the man beside him.

"Ira's and Dean's dads," Kenny told Tu.

"Gee, I'd never have guessed," replied Tu.

Tammy Thompson's father was already there. So were Shayne Bradshaw's parents. They were all talking to Ms Benge and Mr O'Neill and nodding their heads politely.

"Maybe Ms Benge is doing their horoscopes," whispered Tu. "'This is a good day to give your child a new sporting experience'." Ms Benge caught Tu's eye and winked.

A car pulled into the parking lot. Silina Johns climbed out, tossing back her long hair. Kenny's cheeks started changing colour. A woman got out, also tossing back long, fair hair.

"Silina's mum," Kenny and Tu agreed.

Another car pulled up. Murdoch Boyd got out and combed his hair. A man got out of the driver's side. A man with a totally bald head.

"Murdoch's dad?" Tu and Kenny gasped.

Dallas Orr appeared. "Are your par—" Kenny began, but his father interrupted, saying, "Hi, Dallas. Feeling fit?"

Ani Niwa, her dad, and four of her brothers came walking across the field.

"Right," said Mr O'Neill, looking pleased with himself after speaking to the Bradshaws and Mr Thompson. "We're all here, then."

"I'll just go and get those hockey shirts," beamed Ms Benge. "Isn't it nice to see so many parents?"

"Holly isn't here," said Silina, looking around.

"Anyone know where—" Mr O'Neill began, then stopped.

A snarling, roaring noise was coming from the road leading into Jubilee Park. A gleaming black motorbike came down the road and turned into the car park. A figure in black leathers, black gloves, black boots, and a black helmet with a black visor got off.

Another black motorbike appeared, with another figure in black riding it. A smaller figure, also in black from helmet to boots, sat behind, holding onto the rider's waist. The third figure's legs were too short to reach the footrests. All three figures dismounted and took off their helmets and gloves.

Holly's mum had spiky hair like Holly. She had studs in her nose as well as her ears. Mr Potroz had a tattoo on the back of one hand saying DEATH RULES, and one on the other hand saying HI MUM.

"All right, princess. Have a good game, okay?" said her mum.

"Yeah, princess," said her dad. "Just be careful, and don't get hurt, eh."

Then attention switched away from Holly. Ms Benge was hurrying towards them with a black and yellow sports bag. She looked embarrassed.

"I'm afraid we have a bit of a problem, people,"

she said. "I've just looked at these hockey shirts my friend has lent me, and —"

Ms Benge reached into the bag. She pulled out a piece of clothing that was half yellow and half black. She held it up. It had no collar, no buttons, no sleeves. What it did have was pleats and an elastic waistband.

"— she seems to have lent me a whole set of hockey *skirts*!"

The Welton kids just stared, open-mouthed.

Chapter 11

When Mr O'Neill stood up in assembly on Monday to report on the game against Stratton Road, he started to cough.

"He's nervous," whispered Ani to Tammy.

"He's got a cold," whispered Kenny to Tu.

Mr O'Neill coughed again. "The Welton Intermediate School New Image rugby team — the Welton Wonderers — had their first competition game on Saturday against Stratton Road. The Welton Wonderers won by thirty-five points to nineteen. Tries were scored by Ani Niwa," — Ani stared at the seat in front of her — "Shayne Bradshaw," — Shayne stared at his calculator — "and Ira Esera." Ira stared at his feet. "Murdoch Boyd had a very successful game," Mr O'Neill continued, "scoring *two* tries" — a murmur went through the assembly, and Murdoch smiled — "and he kicked conversions for all five team tries." A louder murmur went through the assembly and Murdoch smiled wider.

"Murdoch this, Murdoch that," Kenny muttered as they walked back to class. "He didn't mention how Murdoch missed a tag and the Stratton Road kids scored!"

"And he didn't mention how we had to play in our own T-shirts and things," Dean said. He shook his head, making his glasses wobble. "Hockey skirts!"

"Still, thirty-five to nineteen was pretty good," said Tammy. "Plus my dad says he's happy for me to play, now that he knows what New Image is like."

"Eastern Heights beat St Jude's fifty-seven to twelve on Saturday," Tu announced. "My cousin told me. He said Jay Viliamu and Troy McCracken got two tries each — and they only played half the game. Their team's all boys."

"Fifty-seven points!" muttered Shayne. "That's ... that's one-point-two-eight times as many in one game as we've scored in two games!"

"Mr O'Neill's seen the draw for the whole competition," Kenny told the others. "We don't play Eastern Heights till the last game."

"Wish it was the last game next year," muttered Ani, "then I'd be at high school."

"And," said Tu, "my cuz says that when he told them we had four girls in our team, Troy McCracken said it might make up for all our useless guys."

The Form Twos were silent as they entered Room 14.

Mr O'Neill coughed, sniffed, sneezed and gasped his way through practice on Tuesday and Wednesday afternoons. "We're playing Kaimana Valley School on Saturday," he gurgled on Wednesday, "at Kaimana Valley. Could you all ask your parents if any of them can bring cars, please?"

"How about motorbikes?" asked Tu. Holly stuck her tongue out at him, quickly grabbing her gum before it fell to the ground.

Dallas Orr wasn't at practice on Thursday. Nor was Mr O'Neill. Co-coach Ms Benge took them instead.

"I've got a book about rugby from Mr O'Neill," she told the team, "so let's do some passing practice."

Ms Benge opened the book. "Now — 'Hold the ball with outside hand supporting, four fingers along the seam and thumb gripping the opposite side. The heel of the palm of the inside hand should be braced against the opposite side of the ball, with fingers ready to impart a spiral spin, and thumb securing stability of ball against outside hand ...'"

Ms Benge closed the book and looked blankly at the team. They looked blankly back at her.

"Let's have a practice game instead," she ordered. "How about Pisces, Aquarius, Gemini and Capricorn against the other star signs ... "

"Right, Ms Benge," said Kenny. "Train, don't explain."

Mr O'Neill was back for the Friday team meeting, and a smile was back on his face.

"Good news!" he announced as soon as everyone was there. "We've got a set of jerseys."

"Cool!" "Choice!" "What colour?" "Where from?" came a teamful of voices.

"Mr Esera has borrowed a set of rugby league jerseys," Mr O'Neill smiled. "He's bringing them along on Saturday. Tell him thanks very much, Ira."

Ira was again sitting with elbows on knees, chin in hands, eyes on the floor. "No problem," he rumbled.

"Now — we need a captain for tomorrow's game," Mr O'Neill continued. "I'd like you all to have a turn, and I'd like Murdoch to be captain against Kaimana Valley."

Silina smiled at Murdoch. Murdoch smiled at everyone. Kenny pulled a face at the wall.

Friday afternoon, it started to rain. It rained all afternoon and most of that night. When five carloads of Welton parents and kids reached Kaimana Valley School on Saturday morning (Holly's parents were at the Motorbike Expo), the rain had almost stopped, but a cool wind was blowing.

"Look at the field!" gasped Tammy. "It's a swamp!"

The Kaimana Valley playing field was a brown oblong of mud, with a few grassy tufts poking up and little pools of water lying in the footprints. The field next to it, where another game was just starting, looked almost as bad.

"If we fall over in that, we'll really be All Blacks," said Dean.

"I'll get mud in my hair," complained Silina.

"Never mind," said Tu helpfully. "So will Murdoch."

A voice like a grizzly bear growled from behind them. "You kids better try these jerseys," Ira's father said.

Mr Esera opened the top of a black plastic rubbish bag and began lifting out jerseys three at a time.

"Orange and purple," murmured Ms Benge. "Out of this world!"

Ani and Tammy chose two jerseys exactly the same size. Dean removed his glasses, pulled on a jersey, found his glasses and discovered he'd put his jersey on inside out. Ira just managed to squeeze the biggest jersey over his shoulders. Murdoch refused two jerseys because they were crumpled, then found a neatly folded one. Holly put on the smallest jersey and stood around grinning — it almost reached her knees before she tucked it in.

"Silina — reserve for the first half, please," said Mr O'Neill. Silina looked almost relieved as she watched the others step out onto the muddy field.

The first half was a shambles. Dean passed to Murdoch; Murdoch tried to swerve left, then swerve right. Instead he skidded in the mud and swerved squelch! onto his backside.

Not long afterwards, Ira intercepted a pass, ran a little way, then passed to Tammy. Trouble was, Ira kept sliding in the mud even after he'd passed the ball. He slid for another ten metres, rumbling like a runaway tank and knocking two Kaimana Valley kids flying as he did so.

Suddenly, there was a shriek from one of the Kaimana Valley girls: "Thtop! I've lotht my tooth. My falth tooth."

The game came to a halt while twenty players, plus the Kaimana Valley coach who was refereeing the first half, searched around in the mud. Finally, Shayne held up a small muddy white square with plastic hooks on it.

"Thath it!" exclaimed the Kaimana girl. "My plathtic fantathtic. Thankth." And while the Welton team watched, eyes and mouths round, she wiped the tooth on her shorts and slipped it back into her mouth.

By half-time the Welton Wonderers had scored one try, thanks to Dallas being on the spot when one of the Kaimana Valley girls dropped the slippery ball. Kaimana had also scored a try, thanks to one of their girls being on the spot when Dallas dropped the slippery ball.

"Got any hot pies, Ms Benge?" asked Tu.

"Never mind hot pies," Mr O'Neill said. "Let's have lots of short passes this half. Short passes and calling for the ball like we've practised. It's too slippery to try long passes."

Tu was reserve for the second half, although Silina insisted she didn't mind sitting out the whole game. "It's okay," said Tu. "I haven't got a cousin in this team, anyway."

Mr O'Neill was right. The short passes and calling for the ball worked. People still dropped the ball and slipped in the mud, but good tries were scored by Tammy, Shayne ("Good on ya, tooth fairy!" yelled Tu from the sideline), Murdoch and Ira, who kept on sliding after he'd forced the ball, almost flattening two spectators. Murdoch converted two of the tries despite the wet, heavy ball. Kaimana Valley got one more try, and Welton won 29-14.

The score could have been 34-14. Midway through the second half, Dean got the ball and set off on a curving, swerving, flying run. While the other Welton players yelled and shouted, Dean tore past three staring opposition players and over the goal line. Only trouble was, without his glasses, Dean had made his curving, swerving, flying run across onto the next field where the other game was in progress, and he scored over the next field's goal line.

"You guys are good, all right," Tammy's father smiled as his try-scoring daughter and the others were gratefully putting on warm sweatshirts and jackets after the game was over. "You must be good if you can afford to score tries for other teams as well!"

Chapter 12

"Greenpark on Saturday, at Greenpark," Mr O'Neill announced at practice the following Tuesday. "Got any cousins there, Tu?"

Tu grinned and shook his head.

"I have," said Holly. Everyone looked down at her as she chewed her gum. "She's not in the team, but she reckons they've got one really brilliant guy who scores nearly all their points. The rest are okay. They've lost one game so far."

The rest of the team, meanwhile, were staring at the black leather mittens covered with metal studs that Holly was wearing. "My aunty Charlene gave them to me for Christmas," she explained.

"Princesses in fairy stories only wear *silk* mittens," said Tu.

Holly looked up at Tu and chewed thoughtfully. "Read a lot of fairy stories, do ya?"

"All right, people," interrupted co-coach Benge, trying to hide her grin. "Let's make this a really good practice."

Practice began with everyone dividing into two teams for passing. Ms Benge joined one team to make the numbers even. Two players from each team raced up to halfway, passing a ball backwards and forwards, then raced back again, still passing. Then the next two went, and so on. Murdoch and Ms Benge set off together; Murdoch started off slowly so Ms Benge wouldn't get too puffed, but found Ms Benge was way ahead of him, calling for him to hurry up.

It was a good practice. So were the other two practices that week. Everyone concentrated hard on training, though some of the boys also concentrated on Silina's new glossy black shorts.

Wednesday's practice included a game where everyone stood in a circle around the ball, Mr O'Neill blew his whistle, and everybody had to rush in and see who could grab the ball first. It didn't work particularly well. Everyone except Holly hung back and let Ira go first. Ira, who hadn't thumped anyone for nearly a week, stood back politely and let Holly go first.

Thursday's practice introduced an incredibly cunning move.

"Okay, so we get a penalty kick near the other team's goal line," explained Mr O'Neill. "We all get in a tight circle around the ball. Someone — probably Silina, 'coz she's a fast runner — sticks the ball under their jersey. Everyone runs off in all directions, yelling and pretending they've got the ball. Meanwhile, Silina tiptoes in and scores while the other team wonders what's happening."

"Choice!"

"Yeah, good one!"

"Let's try it!"

The Wonderers got into a circle around the ball. The Wonderers ran off in all directions, yelling and shrieking "Here, Kenny!" "Here, Dallas!" "Here, Ani!"

But ...

"Why is the ball still lying on the ground?" asked Mr O'Neill through tight lips.

"I'm not sticking that under my jersey!" huffed Silina. "It's all dirty and yuk!"

"All right — someone else take the ball," said Ms Benge. "Try it again."

The Wonderers formed a circle around the ball a second time. The Wonderers ran in all directions a second time. The Wonderers yelled and shrieked a second time.

"Why is the ball *still* lying on the ground?" asked Mr O'Neill through even tighter lips.

"You didn't say who should pick it up," an embarrassed voice replied.

"All right ... Dean, you take the ball," suggested Ms Benge. "Come on, let's try it again."

The Wonderers formed a circle around the ball a third time. The Wonderers ran and yelled and shrieked a third time.

"*Why* is the ball *still* lying on the ground?" Mr O'Neill's voice hissed from his squeezed-together lips.

Dean, whose glasses were safely in Ms Benge's pocket, was peering at the ground about three metres away from the football.

"What ball?" he asked.

Chapter 13

Getting to Greenpark on Saturday morning was "like one of those old movies where everyone rips round like battery toys," said Tu.

Tammy and Mr Thompson were supposed to be picking up Ani at her place. But Tammy's sister, who lived with Tammy's mother in another part of town, wanted a lift to her soccer game, so Mr Thompson had to go there first. Meanwhile, Ani forgot that Tammy and her dad were picking her up, and she turned up at the front gates of Welton Intermediate, where everyone else was meeting.

Tammy and her dad finally turned up and left again with Ani and Silina. Mr Esera arrived and went straight back home because he'd forgotten the jerseys. When he returned, he and Ira and Dean and Tu left. Then Ms Benge, who was taking Mr O'Neill, Shayne, Murdoch and Dallas (who looked as if he hadn't slept all night), also left.

Thirty seconds after the last car pulled out,

Kenny arrived, running. Moments before he and his father were due to leave for Greenpark, the phone rang. A friend of Mr Jury's was offering him a couple of days' work. "Can't afford to turn down the money, son," Mr Jury apologised. "Get a move on and you'll catch one of the others at the school."

Kenny didn't catch any of the others. He stood alone on the footpath outside Welton Intermediate's front gates, a Wonderer wondering what to do. Further down the road he could hear a lawn mower revving.

As he stood there, panic rising in his chest, the lawn mower came round the corner . . . and turned into two motorbikes. The figure on the back of one saw Kenny and called out, "Wanna lift, Kenny?"

Mr Potroz pulled up alongside him. "Yeah, hop on, mate. Get the spare helmet out of the panniers, will ya, princess?"

For the first three corners, Kenny sat stiff and scared behind Mr Potroz, holding him so tightly around the middle that he finally gasped, "Let me breathe, mate!" Holly's father had a tattoo on the back of his neck, too, Kenny noticed. A hinge, and the words LIFT TO INSPECT BRAIN.

For the next eight corners, Kenny became more and more relaxed, leaning into the corners just like Mr Potroz. He could feel the wind thudding at him, making his cheeks bulge and his eyes water. He could hear the roar of the engine streaming back behind him. When Holly and her mum came up alongside on their motorbike at a set of traffic lights, they both grinned at him. Holly's mum said something over her shoulder to Holly, the studs in her nose glinting. Holly buried her face in the back of her mother's neck.

The rest of the Welton Wonderers stared, surprised and jealous, when Kenny arrived at Greenpark. "Two bikies in the team, eh?" growled Mr Esera. "We'll have to call you the Welton Thunderers."

The Greenpark team were kicking a ball around. "Bet that's their good player," said Tu, pointing to a tall, fair-haired boy who had just drop-kicked the ball miles downfield.

"He's cute," said Silina. Murdoch and Kenny both scowled.

The Greenpark team was a mixture of boys and girls, just like Welton. The boys and girls were a mixture of sizes, just like Welton. There was the tall, fair-haired boy, and a little girl with red hair who kept jumping up and down. There was a girl with a hearing aid. There were two boys standing together — a long, stringy one with socks falling over his sneakers, and a short, stubby one with socks pulled up over his knees. There was a Chinese-looking girl and an Indian-looking boy.

"I bet they cover all the signs of the zodiac," said the Wonderers' co-coach when she saw them.

The game was a mixture too.

"Can I be fullback both halves?" Shayne asked Ms Benge. "I've worked out the angles to chase that good guy and cut him off."

Three or four minutes into the game, the tall blond boy got the ball and began to run. Shayne ran too — not at the boy, but at a point about five metres ahead of him. The Greenpark boy reached the spot at the same time as Shayne, who tagged him. "Good stuff, Shayne," puffed the other Welton Wonderers.

A minute after that, the girl with the hearing aid got the ball and ran. The stringy boy and the stubby boy ran beside her, each yelling for the ball.

Suddenly the girl stopped. So suddenly that Shayne and Ani and Tammy all shot straight past without being able to tag her. "What did you say?" the girl asked.

"Pass it! Pass it!" both Greenpark boys yelled. The girl did, and the stubby boy scored.

After the restart, Silina and Ira sprinted for forty metres, passing the ball to and fro just as they'd practised it on Tuesday. Silina scored, and smirked at the tall fair-headed boy. A few minutes later, the same boy tagged Silina. She giggled and dropped the ball; he grabbed it and raced half the field for a try.

Just before half-time, Dallas, still looking tired, dodged and sidestepped half of the Greenpark team and scored in the corner.

At the half-time whistle, Welton were ahead 14-12. Holly, reserve for the first half, took off her studded leather mittens, put a new piece of gum in her mouth, and walked on to the field. Two black figures on the sideline waved black helmets and cheered. Dean, who'd been blinking nervously every time Ani and Tammy grabbed him around the middle for a scrum, went off.

At the beginning of the second half, the bouncy little red-haired girl scored for Greenpark after Ira, Murdoch and Tu all looked too embarrassed to tag anyone so tiny. "She's taller than I am!" Holly hissed at them.

Then Murdoch raced away, with Silina backing up and calling, "Here! Here!" The fair-haired boy sprinted at them. Murdoch flipped a pass to Silina. The boy twisted to tag Silina, stumbled, and grabbed her with both arms to stop himself from falling over. Silina giggled again. Murdoch and Kenny scowled.

Mr O'Neill blew his whistle. "Sorry, mate," he

said to the Greenpark boy. "You're not allowed to hold on to anybody in New Image. Penalty against you."

"Awww!" went Silina.

For the next ten minutes of the game, the Welton Wonderers' practices brought results all at once. Ani scooped up a dropped pass, exchanged four passes with Tammy, and Tammy scored.

"Yes!" yelled Mr Thompson from the sideline, then looked embarrassed and mumbled, "Excuse me."

Holly hooked the ball from a scrum and Kenny threw a huge pass to Murdoch, who dodged the Chinese-looking girl and the Indian-looking boy. He saw the blond boy coming, gave him an ugly look, and ran his hardest to the goal line.

Then Welton were awarded a penalty kick near the Greenpark line. Quickly they huddled in a circle, just like at Thursday's practice.

"Oh, no," groaned Mr O'Neill. "Bet they mess it up."

The circle broke. Welton players ran in all directions, yelling and screaming, "Mine!" "Here!" "Me!" "You!" The Greenpark players chased one way then the other, except for the red-haired girl who just bounced up and down on the spot.

"Hey!" called Holly Potroz loudly. Everyone looked. She was standing beside the goal posts, holding the ball. "I've scored a try, haven't I?"

The figures in black on the sideline threw their helmets on the ground, clapped their black gloves together and yelled. "Yeah! Way to go, princess!"

"There's more room in my jersey," Holly explained to Ms Benge while Murdoch took the kick at goal.

With a minute to go, the blond Greenpark glamour boy took a pass and began running. Shayne, measuring angles and directions, sprinted towards the spot where they would meet, then realised the Greenpark boy was running so fast he would beat him.

Shayne made a desperate dive, his hands stretching out to tag the boy's hips. His fingers grabbed cloth, there was a ripping sound, and giggles began from both sides.

At the final whistle moments later, Welton had won by 33-17. The teams giggled, gave each other three cheers, giggled, left the field, giggled, and headed for the cars.

"He should've kept on running," Dean said as they took off their dirty sneakers by the cars.

"Aw! Get serious!" snorted Ani.

"He could still have scored," Dean insisted.

"Yeah?" said Ani. "Let's see *you* score a try in just your jersey and Bugs Bunny underpants!"

"There's room in our car for you, Kenny," Tammy called.

Kenny looked embarrassed. "Actually, if it's all right with Mr Potroz, I'd like to go on the motorbike ..."

"No worries, mate." Holly's father grinned. "Climb aboard. We'll soon have you saving for a Harley, eh?"

Chapter 14

Kenny, Shayne and Tu had just arrived at school on Monday when Ani and Tammy rushed up.

"Hey!" called Ani. "You guys hear about Eastern Heights on Saturday?"

"What? Did they win by a hundred to nil or something?"

"That would mean a try about every seventy-five seconds," Shayne quickly announced.

"No! They didn't win!" Tammy squealed. "They only drew. It was in this morning's paper. Twenty-eight all — against Dobson Intermediate."

"Hey, man!" said Tu. "Those Dobson kids are real mean hoons. I've got a cousin who knows some of them."

Dean Gooch joined the group, with Ira looming beside him and lots of Form One and Two kids getting quickly out of the way.

"Hi," said Dean. "You heard who we're playing this Saturday?"

"Who?" Kenny asked.

"We're playing here, against some lot called Dobson Intermediate," replied Dean. "Hey, what's the matter? What did I say?"

"So maybe Dobson are a really good team," said Ms Benge at Tuesday's practice. "So what? You people are a good team. You can show them that on Saturday."

"My cousin says they're not just good," Tu replied, "they're good and they're rough."

Dean took off his glasses and polished them. Murdoch checked his hair. Ira squared his shoulders. Holly practised a couple of karate chops.

"No use being rough in New Image rugby," Mr O'Neill reminded them. "There's no tackling or anything like that."

The Welton Wonderers trained long and hard on Tuesday and Wednesday. They trained short and hard on Thursday. They practised scrums where Holly hooked the ball back like a springing trap. They practised backing up so that the person with the ball always had someone to pass to. They practised sprinting to scoop the ball up off the ground till they could all do it — all except Dallas, who wasn't at practice either Wednesday or Thursday.

"It's not fair if he doesn't come," complained Silina.

"If he wants to play, he should be at practice," Murdoch agreed. The two coaches said nothing.

At Friday's team meeting, Mr O'Neill suddenly stopped and complained, "Are you people paying attention? You're bouncing about all over the place!"

"I'm nervous," Tammy told him. "My legs keep shaking."

"And my hands keep twitching," Ani added. "They start whenever I think about tomorrow."

Fifteen minutes before the game against Dobson Intermediate was due to start on Saturday morning, there was a row of Welton parents' cars and two motorbikes parked outside the school gates. Tu's parents had come this time; so had Kenny's mother. Only Dallas's parents were missing.

The team had all changed into their orange and purple jerseys (except for Ira, who was still on the sideline searching for the biggest one) when the Dobson team arrived.

The visitors came up the steps to Top Field in a noisy, yelling group. They started pointing and laughing as soon as they saw their opposition.

"It's a team full of girls!" one of them scoffed. Tammy looked grimly at them.

"Hey, look!" another one said when he saw Holly. "They've got a midget playing for them!" Holly stopped chewing gum and glared.

"Yeah," said a third kid pointing at Dean, "and a four-eyes."

Ira, still rummaging through the gear, started growling to himself. The Dobson players all looked towards him. "Look at the big fat guy!" jeered one. Ira stopped rummaging.

Ms Benge was telling Murdoch that his horoscope promised a good day's goal kicking. "It says things will be straight and true," she grinned. She looked at the visitors. "I'd like to send some of them to a distant planet," she murmured.

Mr O'Neill approached the Dobson team. "Hello. Is your coach here yet?" he asked politely.

"We don't have a coach."

"Yeah, we're too good to need a coach!"

"Fancy that," said Mr O'Neill. "Then you won't mind if I referee the whole game, will you?"

As soon as the game began, the Welton Wonderers realised that the Dobson team were good all right. After just three minutes, one boy dodged past the despairing hands of Murdoch, Kenny and Shayne, and raced away for a try. He trotted back, clapping his hands above his head, then took the conversion kick himself. He tried a drop kick and missed. 0-5.

A couple of minutes after that, the Dobson team sent a series of long passes sweeping across field to another boy who sprinted away to score. He also tried a drop kick, but his went over. 0-12.

The three or four Dobson parents on the sideline were yelling: "Go for it, Dobson!" "You can do this lot, no trouble!" "Let's show 'em, Dobson!" The Dobson players were talking and calling among themselves. "Easy," they said. "Ea-sy!"

The Welton team and supporters were silent. Somehow they hung on till half-time. Dobson didn't score any more points. Shayne was in just the right place to make tags. The long legs of Murdoch and Silina carried them all over the field, helping keep Dobson out.

"Keep closer to them," Mr O'Neill urged at half-time. "You're giving them too much room to move. Stick close."

Dallas, reserve for the first half, went on and Shayne came off.

The second half started. Once again, Dobson sent a series of long passes sweeping across field. But this time the Welton Wonderers were keeping closer. Murdoch swooped, seized the pass meant for the final player, and scooted away to score. 5-12. The Welton supporters cheered for the first time.

Murdoch placed the ball ready to kick the conversion.

"No place kicks!" the Dobson players complained. "We're doing drop kicks, so you gotta do drop kicks."

Murdoch looked at Mr O'Neill. "I can't do drop kicks," he muttered.

"I can," said Dallas Orr. He stepped forward, picked up the ball, and drop-kicked it neatly between the posts. 7-12.

There was a roar from Mr Esera on the sideline. "Way to go, Welton! Good stuff!"

"Who's the big fat pig?" said a Dobson boy loudly. Some of the other Dobson players sniggered.

Ira made a growling noise in which the words "My dad" could be heard.

"Yeah?" sneered the boy. "You look like him, too. Two fat pigs."

Ira rushed forward and grabbed the Dobson boy in a headlock.

There was a shrill blast from Mr O'Neill's whistle. "Stop it!" he barked, in a voice that none of the Welton team had ever heard him use before.

Ira stopped straightaway and stared. "Ira, go and stand on the sideline for ten minutes till you've cooled down. And you —" he turned to the

Dobson player "— you can go off, too. I won't have talk like that in this game."

The Dobson boy muttered but went. So did Ira. He wandered around for a bit, then went and stood next to his father. The Dobson boy stayed further down the sideline.

The game restarted. Within thirty seconds the visitors had scored with another ducking, swerving run from one of their fast players, followed by another successful drop kick. 7-19. The Dobson team chanted again. "Ea-sy! Ea-sy!"

No more points for five minutes. Then there was a scrum close to the Dobson line. Holly hooked the ball so hard that it shot right past Tu, who was waiting to get it. Silina saw it lying on the ground in front of her, scooped it up as they had done in practice during the week, passed to Dallas, who flicked it on to a sprinting Murdoch, who shot across the line again. Dallas's drop kick wobbled over the bar. 14-19.

Just a couple of minutes to go. "Back on, you two!" Mr O'Neill called, and Ira and his opponent scrambled onto the field.

Almost immediately, Tammy sent the ball back to Ira from a line-out. Ira threw a pass to his right; a rushed, badly-aimed pass that was much too low for anyone to catch.

Anyone except Holly Potroz. The tiny, spiky-haired, ear-studded, gum-chewing figure caught the ball at about ankle height. She doubled up and slipped under the tag of one Dobson player. As another one came at her with hands outstretched, she dived in a perfect forward roll and forced the ball just over the line. 19-19.

"We do forward rolls like that in karate," Holly explained as she got up. Then she waved at the sideline where two figures in black leather leapt up and down, yelling "Yay, princess! Good one, hon!"

Dallas held the ball carefully, eyed the posts, and drop-kicked a perfect goal. 21-19.

Mr O'Neill's whistle blew. "Full-time," he called, and all the Welton arms shot up in the air.

The Dobson players trailed down the steps, mumbling "Useless ref ... cheats ... fatguts ... " and giving angry looks.

When the visitors had gone, Mr O'Neill and Ms Benge turned to their gasping, sweating, grinning team.

"I'm proud of you," Mr O'Neill simply said.

"Silina was right," Ms Benge added. "You're the wonderful Wonderers!"

Chapter 15

Murdoch Boyd wore his CHAMPION OF CHAMPIONS T-shirt again on Monday morning.

"Champ of champs?" Kenny muttered to Tu. "More like 'chump of chumps', when you think what he's like at schoolwork."

"But we *are* the champs!" protested Shayne, who had been waiting beside the school drive with Dean and Ira. "We beat Dobson Intermediate. Dobson drew with Eastern Heights —"

"Eastern Heights won again on Saturday," Dean interrupted. "Troy McCracken and Jay Viliamu both got tries."

"Yeah, but you get two competition points for a win and only one for a draw," Shayne went on, "so we're a point ahead of Eastern Heights right now. We're leading the competition!"

"We play Nga Tama this Saturday," said Tu. "My cousin at Stratton Road reckons they're not very good. Stratton beat 'em."

"And we beat Stratton!" Kenny said. The five

boys grinned at one another. Ira made a pleased rumbling noise.

Mr O'Neill didn't report to assembly on the Welton Wonderers' win over Dobson Intermediate. Ani Niwa and Tammy Thompson did instead.

"Murdoch Boyd got two tries —" began Ani. The Form Twos turned to look at Murdoch and murmured. "— and Holly Potroz got one try —" The Form Ones turned to look at Holly, and clapped.

"— and Dallas Orr kicked three goals," finished Tammy. The Form Ones and Form Twos turned to look at Dallas, but Dallas wasn't there.

"S'pose you'll be winning the World Cup next," one of the kids jeered as they walked back to class after assembly.

"Yeah, what makes the Welton Wonderers so wonderful?" laughed another. It wasn't a very friendly laugh.

Mr O'Neill beckoned to his New Image players as they filed into Room 14. "I've just had a message from Nga Tama. They want to play us this Wednesday instead of Saturday. There's a big Polynesian festival on this weekend, so they want to play us midweek if they can — okay with you lot?"

"Okay," answered eight voices. Ira rumbled in agreement.

"We can win on any day," Murdoch added. This time there was a rumble from some of the other Room 14 kids who were listening.

About half an hour after class began, a message came for Mr O'Neill and he left the room. Room 14 were having one of their noisy days, and hardly anybody noticed him go.

Ten minutes later another message came, and this time Ira left the room. A lot of kids noticed him go, especially the ones he'd been thumping on the head to pass the time.

Mr O'Neill came back just before interval. He said nothing. Ira didn't come back till after interval. He said nothing either. He just sat with his head down and his fists clenched. He didn't even answer when Dean whispered to him.

At lunchtime Ira stayed in Room 14. He still wasn't speaking. Dean went in to see him, but came out shrugging his shoulders.

When Room 14 came back inside after lunch, Ira still wasn't speaking. He was shouting. Shouting at Mr O'Neill, who had pulled up a chair and was sitting beside him.

"You're always picking on me!" Ira yelled. "Everyone picks on me!" Ira's face was hot and furious.

Mr O'Neill looked pretty warm too. "Listen, Ira," he said. "I'm not picking —" He broke off when he saw the class all standing and staring in the doorway. "Okay, Ira. Let's leave it for now. Think about it for a while."

Room 14 was quiet all afternoon. Dean spent a long time murmuring to Ira, who growled back. When the bell rang, Ira strode off to the bike sheds by himself. The other New Image kids gathered around Dean.

"Ira's in trouble," said Dean in a flat voice. "Those Dobson Intermediate kids reckon he stole a watch last Saturday."

"Aw, no!" Tu exclaimed. "Ira wouldn't do that!"

"He got in trouble in Form One, remember?" Silina said. "Nicking pens and things from desks."

"Yeah, but that was just mucking around," said Ani.

"Yeah, he always put them back," Tammy added.

"When do they reckon he took the watch?" asked Kenny.

"They say it was in their gear on the sideline," Dean said. "The kid didn't realise it was missing till he got home. It's an expensive one — stainless steel or something. They reckon Ira was mucking around near their stuff before the game."

"He was just looking for a jersey," Tu protested.

"They're just jealous because they lost two competition points," Shayne added.

Dean shrugged. "Ira says he never touched their

82

stuff. And he says he's not going to play for a coach who doesn't trust him."

The others were silent for a few seconds. Then Murdoch spoke.

"Do you reckon Mr Esera will still let us use those jerseys, if Ira's not playing?"

"Oh, shut up, Murdoch!" everyone snapped.

A cold wind blew at practice on Tuesday. It blew on nine players only. Ira didn't turn up. Neither did Dallas Orr — again.

"Dallas has missed twenty-one-point-five percent of practices so far," Shayne announced.

Those who did come were in a bad mood. Murdoch spent most of the time picking at a tiny spot on the leg of his trackpants.

"Never mind, Murdoch," said Ms Benge, trying to make a joke of things, "Train, don't stain, eh?" Nobody laughed.

Mr O'Neill sighed. "Look," he said, "I'm sorry about Ira. I'm not saying he took that watch, but he won't even talk about it. I've got to tell the parents of that Dobson boy something."

"Tell him to go and mess up his own team!" Silina snarled, and swung a bad-tempered kick at a muddy old T-shirt lying on the sideline.

A crowd of mostly Form Two kids stayed behind

83

after school on Wednesday to watch Welton's game against Nga Tama.

"Came to see how wonderful you really are," called one, as the team walked up onto Top Field. Ira wasn't there. He'd disappeared straight after school.

The Nga Tama team had an equal number of girls and boys. "Don't think we've got much chance against you lot," their coach grinned to Mr O'Neill while the Welton Wonderers were doing the stretching and warm-up exercises that Ms Benge had shown them. "I hear you're shaping up to be one of the gun teams."

Half an hour later, the gun team had lost, 24-26. The Nga Tama team was whooping and rushing around with delight. The Welton kids were trying to be good losers.

The game had been a disaster. Captain-for-the-day Dean was only half-trying without his friend Ira. Dallas, a sticking plaster on one cheek, was nervy and jumpy. Silina and Murdoch messed up an easy chance for a try early on, and wouldn't pass to each other for the rest of the match.

The others gave it their best, but nothing went right. Ani and Tammy collided twice. Tu, Kenny and Shayne all left it to one another to make a tag, and the Nga Tama girl ran on to score. Holly was penalised for foot-tripping a Nga Tama boy.

("Forgot it wasn't karate," she mumbled.) Meanwhile, every bounce and pass seemed to go just right for the visitors.

"Welton Wonderers!" called one of the Welton Form Two spectators. "Wonder how you ever won anything!"

"Don't worry about it," Ms Benge said as the beaten team shoved their orange and purple jerseys back in the plastic rubbish bag. "We'll blame it on the stars not shining in the daytime. Am I right?"

"Right," a couple of voices muttered.

"I'm not worried, I'm angry!" snapped Silina. "We'd have beaten them if stupid Ira was here."

"And if Dallas Orr came to a few more practices," complained Murdoch.

Silina swung another angry kick at the muddy T-shirt still lying crumpled on the sideline. Her foot sent it flapping across the grass. There was a clatter and a glitter as something fell from its folds. The Welton Wonderers stared at the ground, where a stainless steel watch now lay.

Chapter 16

"Did you talk to Ira last night?" Kenny asked Dean as soon as he saw him on Thursday morning.

"Yeah, what'd he say?" Shayne wanted to know.

"Ira never *says* anything," Tu reminded them.

"Well, I rang him up," said Dean, "but he already knew about the watch. Mr O'Neill had rung him straight away. And he rang Ira's dad at work."

"Good on ya, coach," said Tammy, who had just arrived with Ani.

"He's quite sensible, really — for a teacher," said Ani.

"So Ira's coming to practice tonight," Dean told them. There were pleased murmurs all round. "Oh ... wanna hear the other big news?" Dean continued. "About me?"

"Don't tell me — they're gonna fit you with radar, so you don't have to wear glasses," said Silina, joining the group.

"Nearly," grinned Dean. "I'm getting contact

lenses. I should have them in time for the school disco."

At the mention of the school disco Kenny glanced at Silina, then looked away. Silina didn't notice.

"Contact lenses!" repeated Tu. "Gross, man! Fancy going round with hunks of plastic in your eyes!"

"They reckon if you take them out the wrong way, your eyeballs stick to them and come out too," Ani informed the others.

"And if you go to sleep in them, your eyes start swelling . . ." added Tammy, who had turned pale.

"Nah, that's all rubbish," said Dean, as the bell rang for the start of school. "Anyway, can't be worse than being called 'four-eyes'."

Mr O'Neill wasn't in Room 14. But Ms Benge was there, talking to Ira and Murdoch. She called the other New Image players over. "Mr O'Neill has gone over to Dobson Intermediate to return the watch — and to collect a letter of apology for Ira."

"So he should!" said Ani and Tammy together. Everybody else laughed. Even Ira, looking at his favourite bit of floor, gave a gurgling noise.

"Mr O'Neill really tries hard for you people, you know," Ms Benge said. She blushed and went off to her own classroom.

"Ooo-weee!" grinned Murdoch when she'd gone. "Who's getting stars in her eyes, eh?"

"Oh, shut up, Murdoch!" came the cry.

"Sounds as if Dean will be able to keep both bionic eyes on the ball," Mr Jury said when Kenny returned home on Thursday after delivering 300 FORGET WINTER NIGHTS WITH A GENUINE IMITATION ELECTRIC LOG FIRE circulars.

"Yeah, having contacts will be good for him," Kenny agreed. He fell silent and wandered off to his room. Contact lenses made him think of the school disco. The school disco made him think of Silina. It also reminded him of an incident after practice that day.

As the team had left Top Field, a spiky haircut appeared at Kenny's elbow. "Keddy?" a voice said.

"Sorry?" replied Kenny uncertainly.

Holly shifted the gum into her cheek and tried again. "Kenny? You gonna go to the disco?"

Chapter 17

"How's Ira Esera getting on these days?" Kenny's father asked that weekend.

Kenny, his mind on the disco coming up on Friday and wondering if Silina would dance with Murdoch all night, looked blank for a moment. Then he said, "Oh, good. He still growls away, but he's mostly stopped pushing people around now. He's really fit, too."

"Eastern Heights forty-one, Nga Tama ten," announced Dean in Room 14 on Monday. "And remember, Nga Tama beat us twenty-six to twenty-four."

"Yeah, but that was because we had a bad day," Murdoch protested. "We'll beat them next time."

"Yeah, we've won four competition games and only lost one," Shayne reminded everyone. "We've drawn one non-competition game, and we've scored—" Shayne's fingers darted over his calculator "— we've scored a hundred and seventy-one million points ... no, hang on, forgot the decimal point ... we've scored a hundred and seventy-one points and had a hundred and twenty scored against us."

"You boys always go on about how many games everyone wins and how many points they score," Ani Niwa complained. "Who cares?"

"Yeah," Tammy agreed. "Why can't you just play the game for fun?"

"It's fun winning," said Tu.

"If you're gonna play the game properly, you have to play to win," said Murdoch.

"Yeah," agreed Silina, "otherwise you're just mucking around."

As both sides drew breath to continue, there was an "Ouch!" from Dean. He bent forward with his hands up to his left eye. A small shining circle dropped out of his eye into the palm of one hand.

"Oooh, Dean!"

"Aw, yuk!"

"How revolting!" went a babble of voices.

Dean straightened up, grinning. "I started wearing my contacts on Saturday and I'm still getting used to them." He placed the little plastic circle on the tip of one finger. "Wanna watch me stick it back in?"

Everyone rushed away to their seats, making sounds of disgust.

At practice on Tuesday, Silina dropped the first pass Kenny threw to her. "Geez, Kenny! Throw it straight, can't you?" she moaned. Kenny went red.

"Now, now," said Ms Benge. "Train, don't complain."

Five minutes later, Mr O'Neill showed the team how to fool the opposition with a dummy pass — one where a player pretends to pass the ball, but holds onto it and keeps running. "Remember to swing your arms and shoulders all the way across," he kept saying. "Make it look convincing."

"What's it called again?" asked Murdoch, who had as much trouble with words as he had with Maths. "A dunny pass?"

"Dummy pass, dummy," scoffed Tu before he could help himself.

Five more minutes and the team were practising another crafty penalty move. All of them except Dallas rushed into a line, ready for the ball to be passed from runner to runner. They crouched, waiting, with their hands held out. Instead, the ball was flicked to Dallas who sprinted and dodged towards the goal line.

"Call the move 'Scorpio'," urged Ms Benge.

"Scorpios can attack from all directions. Am I right?"

"Yeah, but I was running left," said Tu. Two people laughed. Eight people groaned.

"We need an expert ducker and dodger," Mr O'Neill said. "Dallas would be good."

"Yeah, but he's not here," said Holly.

"He's never here," grumbled Silina.

"Shouldn't be allowed to play," said Murdoch sulkily.

Without warning, Mr O'Neill hurled the football to the ground, and it bounced away wildly. He pointed at Murdoch, then at Silina then swept his finger around the others. "Look, you lot ... you're supposed to be a team!" he snapped. "A team doesn't whinge and complain about its members. Players in a team help one another or else —" Mr O'Neill looked at the bent heads of Murdoch and Silina again "— or else *they're* the ones who shouldn't be in the team. If you had any idea ..." He trailed off, catching the warning look in Ms Benge's eye.

Tuesday's practice was very quiet after that.

Wednesday's practice started quietly, too. Dallas was back, but he was always quiet anyway. The other kids were quiet because they were still feeling embarrassed after Tuesday's outburst.

Mr O'Neill seemed a bit embarrassed, too, and set out to lighten things up.

"Busy few days ahead for you lot," he said. "Disco on Friday. Game against Huntertown on Saturday — no, I don't know their team, but Greenpark and Kaimana Valley both beat them. Oh, and there's photos and certificates on Friday, of course."

"Certificates?" asked half the Wonderers.

"Photos?" asked the other half. Murdoch hastily began searching his pockets for his comb.

The two coaches laughed. "You all get certificates for being in a New Image team and learning to do the basic things," said Mr O'Neill.

"And you all get photographed for the newspaper," said Ms Benge. "They're doing an article on school rugby, and they're coming here because Mr O'Neill is so beautiful."

Mr O'Neill began to go pink. After a moment, so did Ms Benge. "Hooooo!" went half the team. Holly put two fingers in her mouth and blew a piercing wolf whistle. Murdoch kept searching his pockets.

At Friday's team meeting, the newspaper photographer came and went. She took photos of the whole team holding their certificates. She took photos of Holly Potroz and Ira Esera holding theirs. "Kneel down," she had to tell Ira, "so I can get you both in."

"Go to bed straight after the disco tonight," Mr O'Neill warned the Wonderers. "Remember we've got to be at Huntertown by nine-thirty."

"Hey!" said Tu to Kenny and Shayne as they left Room 14. "I've just realised why Murdoch Boyd's dad is so bald." The other two boys looked at him. "Well, if he combed his hair half as much as Murdoch does, he probably combed it all out!"

All the Welton Wonderers were at the disco, except for Dallas. Holly and her Form One friends danced and jumped around in a way that reminded Kenny of a karate tournament. A couple of times they all came and jumped around near Kenny, and he wasn't sure what to do. At supper time Holly stood next to Kenny, drinking her Coke and chewing her gum at the same time. Kenny still wasn't sure what to do.

Silina danced with Murdoch once, and Kenny looked grim. Then she disappeared to dance with her friends and Kenny looked pleased. Ani and Tammy danced together. Dean was wearing his glasses — "Don't wanna lose a contact lens where it's gonna get stomped on" — and kept bumping into people. Ira made the floor shake around him. Shayne worked out a dance that would measure the area of the assembly hall. Mr O'Neill and Ms Benge danced together several times, until they realised how many kids were pointing and whispering.

"So," said Mr Jury as he picked Kenny and Tu up afterwards, "was it a success then?"

"Sure was, Mr Jury," answered Tu.

"How could you tell?" asked Mr Jury.

"'Coz it was too noisy to hear yourself talk," Kenny told him.

Chapter 18

"...and then Ira got a try, and Tammy got a try ..." Ani stood in Room 14 on Monday morning with a group of classmates gathered around her.

"Yeah, and then Dallas got a try and Ani got a try and Ira got another try," Tammy interrupted.

"Yeah, and Kenny got a try and Holly got a try and Ira got another try!" Ani went on.

"Just about everyone got a try," Tammy said, "except Shayne and Silina, so Mr O'Neill gave them both a kick at goal. Shayne's went straight over."

"Silina's went straight, too," giggled Ani. "Straight along the ground! She just laughed."

"So did the Huntertown team," Tammy added. "They were really good sports. And their tries were good ones, too."

"Fancy them expecting us all to get changed in the same toilets, though. Gross, man!" Ani saw Tu and Kenny walk through the door, and went on, "Tu was really embarrassed."

"I wasn't embarrassed!" protested Tu. Then he saw the grins.

"Three more games till we play Eastern Heights," said Shayne. "If we win those three we'll be just one competition point behind Eastern Heights. And if we beat them too, we'll win the championship."

The Wonderers looked excited. The rest of Room 14 looked bored.

"Hey, Murdoch," called Tu. "Liked your T-shirt in the photo in the paper." The other kids moved away; they'd heard enough about Murdoch and the photo in the paper.

"It was my Australian T-shirt," explained Murdoch, flicking a speck of dust from his sleeve.

"Yeah?" asked Tu. "I didn't know you were a wobbly."

"You mean a wallaby," Murdoch corrected him.

"Nah, I mean a wobbly."

"We want you to decide," said Ms Benge at Tuesday's practice. "You've heard what Shayne's worked out about the last four games. Is that what you want to aim for? To be the champions?"

"Yeah!" cheered Silina, Murdoch, Kenny, Tu, Shayne and Dean. Holly choked on her gum for a second, then cheered too. Ira rumbled. Dallas nodded. Ani and Tammy looked at each other, remembered the tries they'd scored on Saturday, and said, "Yeah."

"Right, then!" Mr O'Neill smacked his fist into his palm. Some of the kids jumped and the coach massaged his hand. "It's St Andrew's here on Saturday. Three good practices."

They had three good practices — almost. Tuesday was good. Wednesday was good. So was Thursday — until the very last minute.

At the end of Thursday's practice Ms Benge said, "Let's try our ball-up-the-jersey penalty one more time. Holly with the ball. Okay . . . go!"

The Wonderers formed a circle. Then they broke up, calling and shouting and running in all directions. Murdoch ran in a direction that took him straight into Ira. Murdoch crashed to the ground, holding his knee and yelling. Ira stood, looking surprised.

"It's all right, Ira," Mr O'Neill smiled. "Not your fault. Train, don't blame."

Only then did people realise Murdoch was really hurt. The two coaches hurried over. Murdoch could hardly stand. He tried to walk, grabbed his knee again, and sat down hard on the ground.

"I knew it!" said Ms Benge. "I saw a shooting star last night. That's often a sign of bad luck. And boy, was I right!"

Murdoch was at school on Friday, but his knee was bandaged and he could walk only slowly.

"Don't anybody else dare hurt themselves before tomorrow," Mr O"Neill said at Friday's team meeting. "We've got no reserves for St Andrew's."

At five to ten on Saturday morning, the team's supporters were lined up on the sideline of Top Field, looking anxious. Murdoch stood among them, looking anxious. Nine players were gathered around Mr O'Neill, looking even more anxious.

There was no sign of Dallas Orr.

"Does anyone know where Dallas is?" Mr O'Neill asked. Nobody did.

"Do you suppose—?" Ms Benge said quietly. Mr O'Neill gave a quick nod.

"We'd lend you one of our players," the little round St Andrew's coach offered, "but we haven't got any spares, sorry."

The nine Welton Wonderers trotted onto the field, headed by captain-for-the-day Kenny. A strong wind was blowing from behind them. Despite what Mr O'Neill had said at practice the previous week, they weren't feeling happy with Dallas.

The game began. Almost immediately, the Wonderers were feeling happy with themselves. The St Andrew's kickoff went straight to Holly,

She ducked under two tags and passed to Silina. Silina's long legs in the glossy black shorts pranced away downfield, while all the boys in the St Andrew's team seemed hypnotised. Tu called for the ball, and Silina passed to him. Tu passed to Dean, who caught the ball perfectly and tore across the line.

"I could see it! I could see it!" Dean exclaimed excitedly as he walked back. "Contacts are choice!"

Meanwhile, the others looked around at each other. Without Murdoch and Dallas they didn't have a goal kicker.

"Give Shayne a go!" called Mr Bradshaw from the sideline.

Shayne looked at his father, then placed the ball on the ground. Muttering "Fifteen metres . . . three metres . . . ten degrees . . . three steps," he moved forward and kicked the ball just under the crossbar. "Fifteen degrees . . . *four* steps," he muttered. His father shut up.

The St Andrew's players attacked. They had two very fast girls in their team, and with only nine players in defence the Welton Wonderers were gasping to stop them.

But they did stop them. Silina bounded backwards and forwards across the field. Shayne muttered figures and distances and cut people off. Tu concentrated so hard he forgot to grin.

St Andrew's couldn't score.

Then Welton were given a penalty.

"Scorpio!" hissed Kenny. The Welton team formed a line and bent over, waiting for a pass. The St Andrew's players tried to decide whether to mark steamroller Ira or lightning-quick Silina.

The ball went to neither; it flicked from Kenny out to Tu, standing by himself. Tu charged through for a try and his grin returned. This time, Shayne converted it.

Twelve points ahead, and Welton relaxed. They relaxed so much that a minute later they were only five points ahead. One of the fast-running St Andrew's girls made a break. She was tagged by Ani but passed to a boy who scored.

Half-time.

The Welton players collapsed on the grass, gasping and heaving.

"I'm stuffed," groaned Tammy.

"I'm dying," groaned Ani.

"I'm dead," groaned Tu.

The second half was even closer. With the strong wind pushing and thudding behind them, St Andrew's ran hard. With one person short, Welton couldn't break through. It was all they could do to keep St Andrew's out. They ran, tagged, passed, backed up, and longed for the final whistle.

The little St Andrew's coach, refereeing the second half, was looking at his watch every few seconds.

Then, disaster. Silina didn't pass the ball when she was tagged. The referee blew his whistle. "Penalty against you, dear," he said.

"I wasn't tagged!" argued Silina.

"Yes you were, dear."

"I wasn't!" Silina said louder, and stamped her foot.

"You were, and I'm giving the penalty ten metres closer to the goal line for backchat," snapped the St Andrews coach.

"Silina! Get back!" called the others. The Welton parents on the sideline were yelling, too. Mr Esera rumbled like a volcano about to erupt.

The nine Welton players crouched, preparing to tag whoever got the ball.

The St Andrew's captain flicked it to one player. Tu tagged. A second player. Ira tagged. A third player. Dean tagged. The Welton parents yelled louder.

The ball went to a fourth St Andrew's player, who passed straightaway — a little, flipped-up pass, back in the direction from which the ball had come. And suddenly there was one of the fast St Andrew's girls, ball in her hands, flying towards the corner.

The Welton players, still heading in the wrong direction, stumbled as they tried to turn. The St Andrew's girl raced on. Only Holly Potroz was between her and the goal line, standing with knees bent like a tiny Karate Kid.

The St Andrew's girl swerved one way. Holly sprang after her. The girl swerved the other way. Holly sprang again. The girl swung arms and shoulders to hurl a pass to a St Andrew's boy who was backing up and yelling for the ball.

Holly sprang after the boy. But he didn't have the ball. The St Andrew's girl had thrown a perfect dummy pass, just like Mr O'Neill had shown the Welton team. She flung herself over the goal line for a try. The St Andrew's kicker calmly converted it.

Full-time, and Welton had lost, 12-14.

"Ah well," sighed Kenny. "There go our championship chances."

"I could kill Dallas Orr!" Silina snarled.

Tammy and Ani looked towards the sideline where a spiky haircut was being comforted by two sets of black leather arms.

"See!" Murdoch said to the girls as he limped past. "Winning does matter!"

Chapter 19

Sunday morning. Shayne, Tu and Kenny were playing a half-hearted game of Doom on Kenny's mum's computer. Tu and Kenny were half-hearted, anyway, since Shayne had already won four games.

"We could've been playing Eastern Heights for the championship in a couple of weeks," Shayne said, gloomily.

"Yeah. Dallas Orr better have a good excuse on Monday," Kenny said.

Tu just shrugged.

Out in the kitchen, Mr and Mrs Jury looked at each other.

Come Monday, however, nobody asked Dallas if he had a good excuse. One look at his white face and his red swollen eyes was enough. Even Silina and Murdoch — who was no longer limping, but still wore a gleaming white bandage on his knee ("Surprised he isn't wearing a war medal," muttered Tu) — were quiet.

Kenny did try to cheer Dallas up with a joke. "Hey, Dallas! You look like you've been on the booze all weekend!"

Dallas walked away.

"Eastern Heights won again on Saturday," Ani reported.

"Who cares?" said Dean.

"They beat Ellendale thirty-two to something," Tammy added, "and they're playing St Andrew's this week."

"Who cares?" said Murdoch.

"Hey, I've got a cousin at Ellendale," Tu announced.

"Who cares?" said Shayne.

The Welton Wonderers weren't looking forward to Mr O'Neill reading out their result in assembly. Most of them stared at the floor when their coach stood up.

Mr O'Neill cleared his throat. Even after eight weeks he still looked nervous when he had to say anything in assembly. Ms Benge gave him an encouraging smile.

"The Welton Wonderers New Image rugby team was narrowly beaten by St Andrew's on Saturday —" Mr O'Neill began. His team kept their eyes on the floor. "— and I want to say how proud I am of them." The players' eyes snapped up from the floor. "Through no fault of their own they had to play one person short, and they almost beat a very good team. It was a fine effort." Mr O'Neill sat down and Ms Benge gave him a second smile.

"Mr O'Neill's going to be a few minutes late," their co-coach announced on Tuesday afternoon.

After doing their warming up exercises, Ms Benge told the team, "Spread out in a bunch." That really confused everybody.

"Are you going to give us another passing lesson, Ms Benge?" joked Tu. The others laughed.

"No," she smiled. Then she looked serious. "But I want to tell you this . . . I know you think I'm only a stargazer who moons around with her head in the clouds —" The kids groaned, then laughed. "— but Mr O'Neill's right about last Saturday. I'm proud of you too. Okay, maybe you can't win the championship now — but keep playing the best you can. For your own sake..." Ms Benge hesitated, "and for Mr O'Neill's sake."

When Mr O'Neill arrived at practice shortly afterward, along with Dallas, the team were standing in a group looking at him.

"You people okay?" he asked, uncertainly.

"Yeah, Mr O'Neill."

"Fine, Mr O'Neill."

"Let's get going, coach."

"Yeah, the season isn't over yet . . ."

". . . and we've gotta beat Ellendale this Saturday."

It was so cold at practice on Wednesday and Thursday that everyone wore jeans or trackpants and extra jerseys. Ani and Tammy wore gloves, and Holly sported her studded mittens and a yellow woolly hat with a pompom.

"Should wear your motorbike helmet," Dean told her. Holly parked her gum inside her cheek, stuck out her tongue, crossed her eyes, put her thumbs to her ears and waggled her fingers at him.

They were fine, freezing practices. Mr O'Neill showed them how to do cut-out passes where they passed the ball right past one player to the next one along.

"Think I'll sit down and have a rest," grumbled Tu after cut-out passes went straight past him three times in a row.

"There's room in our car if you like," Ms Benge told Kenny on Saturday morning.

"It's okay, thanks." Kenny refused to look at Tu and Shayne grinning at him through the back window of Ms Benge's car. Instead he looked at her bumper sticker reading CAPRICORNS GET MY GOAT, and said, "Holly's already asked if I want to go on the back of her dad's bike."

The game against Ellendale was a jerky one at first. Silina had a chance to score following a good run by Murdoch, but she was busy fixing her headband and dropped the pass. To everyone's surprise, Murdoch just grinned at her. A bit later Holly also had a chance with a pass from Ira, but she was looking at Kenny and missed the ball, too. "Bad luck, princess," called two voices from the sideline.

Gradually, the Welton Wonderers warmed up. Ellendale were a strong team, with twin boys who were excellent dodgers. "I didn't know there were two of them for a while," said Dean at half-time. "I thought there was something wrong with my contacts."

At half-time the scored was tied, 14 all. Tries for Ellendale to one of the twins and their captain, Tu's cousin. Tries for Welton to Kenny and Murdoch. Murdoch was playing really well, with an even bigger clean white bandage on his knee. He'd converted both tries and combed his hair after each one.

In the second half, Welton played some of their best rugby of the season.

They were awarded a penalty, captain-for-the-day Silina called "Scorpio," and while everyone else lined out one way and crouched for the ball, Tammy flicked it to Dallas, who dodged both twins and scored. Minutes later, Holly threw a perfect dummy pass, just like the one that had fooled her the previous week, and scored too. Murdoch converted both.

Ellendale scored again.

Then Murdoch made another good run, passed to Kenny, called for the ball as Ms Benge had told them, got the ball back and made another run. He saw Ira and Dean out to his right and, as an Ellendale defender sprinted to cover Ira, Murdoch sent a long cut-out pass skimming past Ira and into Dean's waiting hands.

Dean shot off ("— like a cat with six Rottweilers after him," Tu described it later). He sped down the sideline, knees lifting, teeth clenched, ball under one arm, other arm pumping. Halfway to the goal line he suddenly swerved wildly and clapped a hand to one eye. He kept on going to the goal line, forced the ball, and trotted back blinking.

"Ran so fast my eyes started watering," he explained. "Thought I was gonna lose a lens."

Again Murdoch kicked the conversion. Welton Intermediate 35, Ellendale 21.

"We'll still give Eastern Heights a fright when we play them," Murdoch promised.

After lunch that day, Kenny told his father about

his discovery on the way home. "Holly Potroz's mum has got a tattoo, too!" he blurted. "I saw it when she took her gloves off. It's a little heart on the back of her hand with Holly's dad's name in it."

"Don't go giving your mother ideas," Mr Jury warned, laughing.

The phone rang and Kenny answered it.

"Hey, Kenny!" Shayne babbled. "Hey, Kenny! Do you know Silina Johns' phone number?"

"What do you want Silina's number for?" Kenny asked suspiciously. Not Murdoch *and* Shayne, he was thinking.

"I want everyone's phone number!" Shayne rushed on. "Eastern Heights —"

"How much did they beat St Andrew's by?" Kenny interrupted.

"They didn't!" Shayne yelled in his ear. "I mean, they did, but they didn't. Eastern Heights won the game thirty-eight to fourteen, but they were a player short and stuck a high school kid in their team — Troy McCracken's brother — they've been disqualified!"

"That means . . ."

"Yeah!" exclaimed Shayne excitedly. "I've checked it on my calculator. We've still got a chance at the championship!"

Chapter 20

"You're absolutely sure?" said Mr O'Neill on Monday morning.

"Sure I'm sure!" Shayne said. "I checked and double-checked and triple-checked everything on my calculator and my computer!"

"And I rang up all my cousins to check their results," added Tu.

"We've won six competition games and lost two," Shayne went on. "That's twelve competition points. Eastern Heights have lost one by disqualification and drawn one against Dobson Intermediate. That's thirteen points. Dobson have got eleven, St Andrew's have got ten. If we win this Saturday, then our last game — the one against Eastern Heights — that'll decide the championship."

"Who do we play this Saturday?" Murdoch wanted to know.

"St Jude's — at St Jude's," Mr O'Neill told them.

"St Jude's?" repeated Silina. "We drew with them in that non-competition game."

"Yeah, but we've got better," Dean pointed out. "I didn't have my contact lenses then."

"St Jude's have probably got better too," Ani pointed out.

"Eastern Heights still reckon they'll waste us, my cousin says," Tu told the others. "They said they'll massacre a team with so many girls in it."

Four girls' faces looked angry and mean.

Ever since New Image rugby had started, Room 14 had become quieter. This week, it was quieter still. Partly because half the kids were thinking about Saturday's game, and partly because of Dallas Orr.

"Why won't you tell us what the matter is?" Tammy begged the coaches when Dallas didn't turn up to Tuesday's practice.

"He always looks so . . . sad," said Ani. "Isn't there something we can do to help?"

Coach and co-coach looked at each other. "I guess it's really up to Dallas," Ms Benge said. "He's the one to tell you."

Room 14 was quiet for other reasons, too.

Silina was quiet because she'd come second to Shayne in last Wednesday's Maths test, and she was working hard to be first again next time.

Murdoch was quiet since Ani and Tammy had laughed at him when he wore his WORLD'S GREATEST LOVER T-shirt to practice on Tuesday.

"Train, don't be vain," they told him.

Kenny was quiet because Holly and some of her Form One friends had begun eating their lunch each day just along from where the Room 14 kids sat. And when Kenny said something after Thursday's practice about the tattoo on Holly's mum's hand, Holly pushed her gum to one side and said, "They started going together when they were really young. Dad's a year older than Mum. How old are you, Kenny?"

"I've got to deliver some circulars," Kenny gabbled, dashing off to collect his 300 copies of WIN A TRIP TO DISNEYLAND WITH JUST 5000 EZY-CHU BREAD WRAPPERS.

Tu followed, trying not to laugh.

"Pass! Pass! Pass!" Mr O'Neill urged the Wonderers at Tuesday's practice. "Call for the ball like we practised. Pass it like we practised. Try dummy passes and cut-out passes like we practised. Keep the ball, don't make mistakes, and we'll score against St Jude's this Saturday, and Eastern Heights next Saturday."

At Wednesday's practice, Mr O'Neill wanted to divide the Wonderers into two teams. "Dry star signs against wet star signs!" called Ms Benge, and laughed at the row of blank faces.

The idea was that one person from each team

would sprint to a rugby ball lying on the ground. The first one there had to scoop it up and pass the ball to the next person in their team without being tagged. When it was Kenny's and Ira's turn to run, Ira did something he hadn't done for weeks. He deliberately barged into Kenny and sent him staggering.

"Leave Kenny alone!" shrilled an angry voice. Holly strode forward, stopped in front of Ira and glared up at him, hands on hips. "Y'sposd—" She took out her gum and tried again. "You're supposed to help people in your team, not hurt them."

Ira looked from Holly to Kenny, and back to Holly. Nobody else moved a muscle — except Tu, who put his arms up over his head and pretended to hide. Ira looked back at Kenny. "Sorry," he grunted.

Plenty of friends and family turned up on Saturday morning to see the Welton Wonderers play St Jude's. Ira's father somehow squeezed into Ms Benge's car. So did Silina's mother, with a scarf covering her long hair. She chattered away to Mr Esera, and Mr Esera rumbled away to her.

Three of Tu's sisters and three of Ani's brothers came. So did Mr Thompson, Mrs Bradshaw, Mr

114

Boyd with the bald head, and Mr Gooch with the glasses.

"Great day!" chirped Mr Gooch, tripping over a parking barrier and colliding with Mr Boyd. "I'm really looking forward to this game," he added, picking up his glasses from the ground."

"Why doesn't your dad get contact lenses, too?" Kenny asked Dean.

Dean laughed. "He enjoys wearing glasses. Keeps saying he can keep an eye on people with them."

And there was another parent at St Jude's, too. One they hadn't seen before. Dallas Orr's father was standing on the sideline. Mr Orr was small and quiet-looking, like his son. He was with another man about the same age.

Kenny had come with his father. Holly Potroz's father was at work, so only one motorbike arrived. "No, we can't fit two people on the passenger seat," Kenny heard Holly's mother say.

"Your dad come to cheer for the winners, eh?" Tu grinned at Dallas. Dallas didn't smile.

Last time the Welton Wonderers had played St Jude's, they were nervous because it was their first-ever game. This time, there were just as nervous because they knew they had to win to have a chance at the championship.

St Jude's were a lot better than they'd been nine games ago. They came at Welton early on, fast and hard, passing and calling just as Mr O'Neill had coached Welton to do. Shayne slipped on a muddy patch as he went to tag a St Jude's girl, and she raced away to score. The Welton Wonderers looked even more nervous.

"Pass! Pass!" Ms Benge called.

"Keep the ball!" Mr O'Neill called.

Slowly, Welton settled down. In the scrums, Holly hooked the ball like a small spiky snake, and the team finally began doing what they'd practised. They kept the ball away from St Jude's with pass after pass, and waited for gaps to appear.

The gaps did appear. Silina raced through for a try after a cut-out pass from Kenny. She gave him a big smile as she walked back, and Kenny dropped his next two passes. Ani and Tammy did another of their Ani-Tammy-Ani-Tammy passing runs, and Ani scored.

The St Jude's defence tightened up and there were no more holes. It didn't stop Dallas, who dodged and ducked and dummy-passed through a half-gap for a try that had spectators from both sides clapping and cheering. Mr Orr stayed quiet.

Captain-for-the-second-half Ani ("I'm only going to be captain if Ani's captain for the second half," Tammy had said at the start of the game) scored another try soon after half-time. Her brothers on the sideline went ape.

Then St Jude's came back with a clever penalty move. They flicked the ball left — one pass, two passes, three passes. The fourth player immediately whipped the ball back to the right, straight into the hands of Tu's cousin who came tearing up from the back and sped through to score. Tu's sisters all cheered, while Tu waved desperately at them to shut up.

Welton swept back, and the last ten minutes brought tries for Shayne, Ira and Murdoch. St Jude's scored again, but the Wonderers were clear winners.

"Forty-five to twenty-one!" Kenny panted as they straggled off the field. "Might give Eastern Heights something to think about."

"Eastern Heights beat St Jude's fifty-seven twelve, don't forget," Shayne reminded him. "Might make them think they're twenty-one points better than us."

Dallas joined the group. He'd gone to speak to his father as soon as the game finished but now Mr Orr and the other man were walking away.

"Did your dad and his friend like the game?" Kenny asked.

Dallas lifted his head. He looked at Kenny, then at the rest of the team. He seemed to be making up his mind about something. "He's not Dad's friend," he said in his quiet voice. "He's a

117

policeman. My father . . . my father's going to jail." And, standing there on the St Jude's field, Dallas began silently to cry.

Chapter 21

"We weren't sure if you knew," Mr Jury told Kenny over lunch. "We didn't want to say anything in case Dallas and the school were trying to keep it private."

"Mr O'Neill and Ms Benge knew about it, I think," said Kenny. "And we all knew something was wrong, but nobody told us what. I still don't know. What's Mr Orr done?"

Kenny's parents looked at each other.

"He's been stealing from the office where he works," said Mrs Jury, "pocketing cheques and money from customers for himself."

"Why?" Kenny wanted to know.

"Mr Orr is an alcoholic," his father told him. "He can't stop drinking — it's like a drug to him. He started stealing to buy more drink."

Kenny remembered the joke he'd made to Dallas about being on the booze all weekend. His face went hot at the thought.

"Dallas and his mum left home about a month

ago," Mrs Jury went on. "Mr Orr was getting violent, I believe."

Kenny remembered Dallas's red eyes, the sticking plaster on his cheek and the bruise on his thigh.

"When the manager at the office found out what he was doing, Mr Orr promised he'd stop. Everyone tried to help him. Basically, he's a decent guy," explained Kenny's father. "Dallas thinks the world of him. But when the stealing started up again, the manager went to the police."

Kenny nodded. He wished someone would give him a hug. He wished Dallas was there so he could say something friendly to him. He wished he'd been like Silina, at St Jude's. It was she who came up to Dallas as he stood crying in the middle of the rugby field, and led him over to Ms Benge. The teacher put her arms around the shaking, small boy and held him tight, while Mr O'Neill quietly shooed the others away.

"You were really good with Dallas," Tammy told Silina while the team waited to. see who was going home in which car.

"Silina's good at everything!" said Ani, smiling to show she wasn't being sarcastic.

Silina looked over to where her mother was talking with Ms Benge, who still had her arms around Dallas. "My father left Mum when I was eight. I kind of know how lonely Dallas feels." She hesitated. "I'm not good at everything," she said. "I'm not good at making friends."

There was a message on the board in Room 14 on Monday morning, in Mr O'Neill's handwriting:

NEW IMAGE CHAMPIONSHIP!
THE BIG GAME!
Welton Wonderers vs Eastern Heights
HERE, NEXT SATURDAY!

Beneath, in smaller letters, was another message in Shayne's handwriting:

Results from last Saturday:
Welton 45, St Jude's 21;
Eastern Heights 64, Kaimana Valley 17.

"Jay Viliamu got four tries for Eastern Heights," Shayne told the others. "Four!"

"We'll be having a proper referee on Saturday for the final," Ms Benge announced at practice on Tuesday. "The Rugby Union's providing one."

"You mean — like on TV?" asked Holly. "One of those referees all in white?"

"Well, I suppose we could lend him one of our purple and orange jerseys," joked Mr O'Neill, "but Eastern Heights mightn't be very impressed."

Nobody laughed. There were still five days before the game, but the Welton Wonderers were already feeling nervous.

"My cousin says Eastern Heights are picking their strongest team to play us," Tu told the others.

"Do you guys want to do that?" asked Ms Benge. "Have the best players on for the whole game?"

The Welton Wonderers looked uncertainly at one another. Finally, Holly shifted her gum and said, "I'm the smallest. So I could be the reserve."

"No, Holly!" came a chorus of voices.

Dallas spoke shyly. "Well I've missed a lot of practices so I—"

"No, Dallas!"

Dean gestured weakly. "My eyes—"

"No, Dean!"

A rumble came from Ira Esera. The others stared at him. Not Ira! They had to have Ira! "We're a team," he growled. "We all play."

The Wonderers' heads nodded like balloons on strings. Mr O'Neill grinned. "Good one, Ira. We'll draw straws on Friday to find a reserve for each half. And to see who'll be captain."

"The stars are looking very interesting this weekend," Ms Benge added. "Mars is really bright, and that usually means war. Am I right?"

"Too true," Tu agreed. "It'll be war, all right."

Chapter 22

On Wednesday morning in Room 14, Murdoch slipped a note to Silina. Kenny saw him and glared. Silina read the note and giggled. Kenny glared harder. Then Silina slipped the note to Shayne, who read it and grinned. Kenny stopped glaring and looked puzzled.

The note went from Shayne to Dean to Ira to Ani to Tammy. Each of them read it, grinned, and passed it on. Finally, just as Kenny thought he would burst, the note reached him.

In Murdoch's scrawl, it said: Dad saw Mr On'eill and Ms Benje at the moveis last nite. They were holdeing hands. Kenny grinned too, and slipped it on to a waiting Tu. Tu read it, grinned, scribbled something on the note, and passed it back to Kenny. Kenny read the new words: Maybe they're in training too! and sniggered.

A hand reached over Kenny's shoulder and seized the note. As Kenny stared at his desk and his ears turned taillight red, a voice murmured

"Hmmm," and a ballpoint scribbled. The note was returned to Kenny's desk.

While Kenny read the new words: Mr O'Neill is the coach. Ms Benge is the co-coach. Tu and Kenny can write this out 30 times, Mr O'Neill strolled back to his desk, smiling to himself.

At practice on Tuesday, everyone had been so carefully nice to Dallas that no one had wanted to tag him. They'd all smiled politely while Dallas ran past them.

They didn't do the same at Wednesday's practice. Dallas wasn't there.

"No, I don't know why," said Mr O'Neill, "but we can probably guess."

"Being in this team has been great for Dallas," co-coach Benge added. "I know some of you weren't happy when he kept missing practice" — several Wonderers looked embarrassed — "but let's help him end the season on a good note."

"He can score all my tries against Eastern Heights this Saturday," Tu offered.

The coaches worked the Wonderers hard at practice. They made them pass and run to back up the person they'd passed to, pass again, run and back up again. "Same as against St Jude's," Mr O'Neill called. "Our team keeps the ball, so our team does the scoring."

Then the Wonderers planned how to defend if Eastern Heights were attacking. The two fastest runners, Murdoch and Silina, practised guarding a sideline each. "We mustn't let people like Jay Viliamu and Troy McCracken have room to swerve outside us," Ms Benge urged.

The rest of the team practised more backing up; backing up taggers this time. "If an Eastern Heights player dodges one of you, there should be someone else there to tag them," said Mr O'Neill.

"I think I'm too old for this," groaned Tu as they came puffing off Top Field after Wednesday's practice. But he grinned as he groaned.

"It's going to take a good team to beat you lot," were Ms Benge's parting words.

It was raining on Thursday morning, so Kenny wasn't surprised to find that the school corridors were full of kids. He was surprised to find those kids gathered around huge posters decorated with stars and moons and zodiac signs, and he was surprised and embarrassed to see what was on the posters.

"Ms Benge?" asked Ani.

"Who else!" agreed Tammy.

The Wonderers remembered the sneers from the other kids when they lost to Nga Tama. They waited for the posters to bring more sneering.

THE STARS ABOVE SAY

"Come and See the Stars Below

in Action!"

New Image Rugby Championship

WELTON WONDERERS

vs EASTERN HEIGHTS

Top Field, Saturday, 10 a.m.

Let's Have a Galaxy of Supporters

and Eclipse the Opposition!

But, to their relief, everyone seemed friendly.

"Good luck, you guys," voices in the corridor encouraged them.

"Yeah — make sure you thrash Eastern Heights!"

"Hey! They like us!" exclaimed Kenny.

"Maybe they just don't like Eastern Heights," Tu said.

In Personal Writing on Thursday morning, Mr O'Neill told Room 14, "Right — quick thinking time. Everything you can scribble in fifteen minutes, beginning 'There were only sixty seconds left ...'"

Fifteen minutes later, Mr O'Neill gathered up the papers. Murdoch's was on the top: *There were onley sixty seconds left in the New Immage Champoinship. We were loosing 28-35 ...*

Mr O'Neill looked at a side each of scribbles and crossings-out from Ira, Kenny and Tu. He looked at a side-and-a-half each from Tammy, Ani and Dean. He looked at two perfectly neat, perfectly spelt sides from Silina, and two perfectly neat, perfectly spelt and perfectly word-counted sides from Shayne. Every single one began: *There were only sixty seconds left in the New Image Championship ...*

"You people got something on your minds?" asked Mr O'Neill.

It was still raining after school on Thursday. "Train, don't rain!" Dean yelled at the sky.

The coaches met the team standing in the doorway of the assembly hall, glaring at the leaden sky.

"We can't practise on Top Field," Mr O'Neill said, gloomily. "It'd ruin it for Saturday."

"But we've gotta practise!" wailed Tammy.

"Yeah — it's our last chance," agreed Ani.

Ms Benge gazed back out the door. The rain was easing off. "Why don't we go on the netball courts?" she suggested. "We can still practise moves and passing there."

Three minutes later, the rain had stopped completely and the Wonderers were splashing around on Welton Intermediate's asphalt netball courts. Kids wandering home down the school drive looked at them and shook their heads.

"A careful, thoughtful last practice," ordered Mr O'Neill. "No bruises or broken bones. Just think about what you know."

The Wonderers practised scrums, with Holly hooking "like a bikie blur", as Tu described her. They practised passing, backing up and calling. They practised defending and backing up while Silina and Murdoch guarded the sidelines. They practised dummy passes and cut-out passes. They practised their penalty move with the ball hidden up Holly's jersey. "Aaarghh! It's all wet and cold!" yelled the ball-holder, losing her chewing gum into a puddle.

They did their Scorpio move, where everyone got into a line waiting for the ball, and the ball was flicked the other way — to Dallas Orr, back at school this Thursday, who sidestepped and dodged Mr O'Neill and Ms Benge all the way down the netball courts.

"Choice, Dallas!" Everyone applauded, and Dallas smiled and blushed. Ira thumped him on the back to congratulate him, and Dallas gasped and staggered.

Finally, the Wonderers had a quick game among themselves. It lasted only five minutes, and ended with Silina sprinting for the line with just Holly in front of her. As Silina drew nearer, swerving and dodging, Holly crouched, gave a piercing karate yell... and stamped one foot in a huge puddle.

Water sprayed up all over Silina's face and hair. Silina gasped and dropped the ball, then chased Holly right around the court and all the way to the girls' toilets. The rest of the Welton Wonderers went giggling after them.

"Did you do every letterbox?" Tu asked Kenny later, as they biked home after delivering 300 circulars reading: PUT A GLOW IN YOUR PET'S LIFE. USE OUR NEW LUMINOUS FLEA COLLAR!

"I dunno," Kenny replied. "I kept forgetting what street I was in!"

"Me too," Tu told him. "I met Shayne down the road, and he said there's only thirty-nine and a quarter hours till the final..."

"Okay, so we'll all meet here — in this room — tomorrow morning at half past nine," Ms Benge announced at Friday's team meeting. "We'll have a team talk before the game."

The Welton Wonderers nodded. Holly chewed her gum harder. The strain was beginning to tell. Ira chomped his way through a doughnut. "He always eats when he's nervous," Dean said.

The team drew straws to see who would be captain on Saturday. "It's me," said a quiet voice, and everyone felt pleased for Dallas.

They drew to see who would be reserve for each half. Tu got the first straw. "I'll be faster than anyone else in the second half," he promised.

Dean got the second short straw. "I'll be able to keep an eye on you from the sideline," he said. "In fact I'll keep four eyes on you."

"Right. A good sleep tonight, everyone," said Ms Benge. "I'll check on the stars for you." No one laughed.

"And no bungy-jumping or BMX riding tonight," Mr O'Neill joked. "I don't want any legs in plaster tomorrow." Still no one laughed.

Mr O'Neill looked at the grim, nervous faces in front of him and raised his eyebrows. "Go away!" he told them.

Kenny went to bed that Friday night earlier than he'd done since he was about eight years old. Thirteen and a half hours till the final. But he couldn't sleep. He turned on his light and tried to read. He was starting to feel drowsy and thinking about turning his light out again when the phone rang.

Mr Jury answered it. "Hello? . . . Yes? . . . Yes . . . Oh no!. . . No, we've seen nothing. . . Of course we will . . . If there's anything I can do . . . Of course . . . Righto, bye."

Kenny heard footsteps coming down the hall towards his room. His father opened the door. "That was Mrs Orr," he told Kenny. "Dallas has run away. . ."

Chapter 22

On a blue and yellow Saturday morning, ten white-faced Welton Wonderers gathered in Room 14. There was half an hour to go till the championship final.

"Ms Benge is with Dallas's mother," Mr O'Neill told the rest of the team.

"So's my mum," said Silina, sitting with Ani and Tammy. Since the previous Saturday, when Silina had been so good to the upset Dallas, the twosome had become a threesome.

"Does anyone know where—" Kenny began.

Mr O'Neill interrupted him. "No. Dallas vanished after tea last night. He left a note on his bed saying he wanted to see his father."

The Wonderers' coach paused, then added: "Mr Orr went into prison yesterday." The team was silent. Mr O'Neill continued. "Without Dallas, we've got no reserves. Tu and Dean, you'll be playing both halves of the game."

"Mr O'Neill?" Murdoch said. "Dallas was going to be captain."

"I know," their coach replied. He paused again. "I want Ira to be your captain for the championship final."

Ira had come in nibbling a muesli bar. "I know you eat when you're nervous, Ira," Mr O'Neill had said, "but I don't want you weighed down so you can't run." So for the past few minutes Ira had been nibbling his fingernails instead.

Now Ira lifted his head and looked at Mr O'Neill. "Okay," he rumbled. Then he looked around at the others, who listened in amazement to the sound of Ira making a speech. "We're gonna win this game for everyone here at Welton Intermediate," he growled. "We're gonna win this game for Dallas."

"My hands are sweating," Kenny said five minutes later, when the team was all changed and waiting to go up to Top Field.

"My mouth is dry," Dean told him.

"There're cars parked right along the road outside school," Silina said. Murdoch took out his comb for the third time in two minutes.

"All my brothers have come," said Ani. "I told them I'd thump them if they didn't." Murdoch put away his comb.

"I spent half an hour on my computer last night,"

Shayne announced. "I worked out the exact places to be when I'm defending. It says I have to be in five-and-a-half places at once!"

"My legs are twitching," Tammy told everyone.

"I have to go to the loo again," Tu chipped in.

Holly stuck a piece of gum in her mouth and found there was already one there. "Good luck, you guys," she said.

The black and green jerseys of Eastern Heights were already on Top Field when the Welton Wonderers came up the steps in their purple and orange. Kenny recognised Jay Viliamu and Troy McCracken straight away. He also recognised the boy who had smashed his softball pitch out of the field. He heard the Eastern Heights boys talking about them. "That's Murdoch Boyd . . . there's the little bikie kid — Polly or Holly or something . . . Ira Esera's the big guy . . ."

There was a crowd of spectators on Top Field. The Wonderers gasped when they saw people standing two and three deep along both touchlines.

The boys from Eastern Heights were looking at the crowd, too. "There's a bikie gang here!" Kenny heard Jay Viliamu say, and followed his gaze to the sideline where he saw the familiar two figures in black leather, plus three or four others similarly dressed.

Kenny's mum and dad stood nearby. ("'Course I'm not doing any work today!" Kenny's father had snorted.)

Kenny could see Mr Esera, too. As usual, he was easy to see — and to hear. "Come on the Wonderers!" he was booming already.

A young, dark-haired woman in white shorts and rugby jersey approached the two teams. "Hi there," she smiled. "I'm Karla Patu, your referee."

Ira shook hands with Troy McCracken, the Eastern Heights captain.

"Twenty minutes each way, right?" said the referee, and tossed a coin. "Welton call."

"Heads," growled Ira. It was tails.

"We'll play with the wind, first half," said Troy, and licked his lips.

Tu and Kenny looked at each other. For the first time they realised that the Eastern Heights boys were nervous, too. In spite of his sweating hands, in spite of the missing Dallas, in spite of everything, Kenny felt a great rush of excitement surge up inside him.

The first five minutes of the New Image Rugby Championship were jerky, anxious ones for both sides.

"Back up! Back up!" Mr O'Neill hissed as the Wonderers trotted onto the field. Kenny, whose mind kept whirling like a runaway comet (must be Ms Benge's star talk rubbing off on him, he thought), wondered for a second if their coach was wanting them to reverse down the field. Then he remembered what they'd talked about at practice.

The Welton Wonderers did back up. Whenever one of them had the ball, another was supporting and calling out. Whenever Eastern Heights had the ball, two Wonderers were there to make the tag. Silina and Murdoch guarded the touchlines against the opposition's fast runners. Troy McCracken and Jay Viliamu weren't just fast, they were good-looking as well, Kenny noted jealously. But Silina was concentrating too hard to notice.

The first scrum went down. The Welton front row of Ani, Holly and Tammy glared at the all-male Eastern Heights front row so fiercely that the boys hesitated. Holly hooked the ball back in a gum-chewing flash. Ira took it and threw a huge, long, enormous, one-handed pass halfway across the field to Dean, just like he had in the first game against St Jude's. Dean caught it perfectly, yelled "Contact lenses!", much to the bewilderment of the Eastern Heights player marking him, and raced almost to the goal line before Jay Viliamu tagged him. The crowd yelled and cheered.

Ani dropped a pass. The Eastern Heights softball smasher snatched it and began to run. But Silina was backing up Ani and she was able to tag him. The two Welton girls grinned at each other.

Then, suddenly, things went wrong for Welton.

Troy McCracken got the ball. He dodged Holly's tag. Tammy was backing up and, quite accidentally, Troy dodged straight into her. Tammy went sprawling. When she got up, she was limping.

"Sorry," panted the Eastern Heights captain, looking embarrassed.

"I'm okay," said Tammy. But she wasn't. She could move only at half speed. "I can't go off," she told the others. "We haven't got any reserves." The rest of the team looked worried.

Within two minutes they looked more worried. An Eastern Heights player sprinted up one sideline with Jay Viliamu beside him. Murdoch, guarding the sideline, saw another purple-and-orange Welton jersey backing up, and went straight for the boy with the ball. But the Welton jersey was Tammy, trying to hobble across. Jay Viliamu took the pass, swerved easily outside the limping girl, and tore away to score. The Eastern Heights kicker, wiping nervous hands on his shorts, placed the ball and missed the conversion. 0-5.

With Welton down to just nine fit players, Eastern Heights started finding gaps to run through. Silina and Murdoch were having to leave the sidelines to back up their team-mates.

Another three minutes and Eastern Heights attacked down the centre of the field, passing and calling and backing up just as Welton had learned to do. While the purple-and-oranges scrambled to tag them, a pass shot out to Troy McCracken. He sprinted down the side of the field that Silina had left unguarded, just beat Shayne, who was defending in three of the five-and-a-half places he needed to be in at once, and was in for his team's second try. This time the conversion went over. 0-12.

The Welton supporters were quiet.

Again Eastern Heights attacked. Again they sent a long pass out towards the sideline — Murdoch's sideline. But this time, a long-haired, long-legged figure came racing across from the opposite sideline, snatched the ball out of the air, and flashed away for a try before the crowd had even begun cheering.

"Good one, Silina!" the Wonderers told her. "We can score! We can win!" they told one another.

Murdoch the kicker wiped his sweaty hands on his shorts and kicked a perfect conversion. 7-12.

As the Wonderers waited for Eastern Heights to

kick off again, Tu's face suddenly opened in a vast grin. "Look!" he said, pointing.

A new group of figures was on the sideline. Dallas Orr stood with his mother, Ms Benge and Mrs Johns.

Seventeen minutes of the half gone. Another Eastern Heights attack. "Yes!" yelled the softball smasher as he and a team-mate had only Shayne to beat.

"*Yes!*" yelled Tu at the same time, even louder — and the Eastern Heights player threw the ball to Tu by mistake. The referee looked thoughtful and awarded Eastern Heights a penalty, while Tu tried to look sorry.

Nineteen minutes gone. Yet another Eastern Heights attack. Holly made a desperate tag. The Eastern Heights boy flicked the ball to another. Holly, her body still leaning towards the first boy, jumped in the air and tagged the second boy with a perfect karate kick. While he hesitated, the hobbling Tammy arrived and tagged him properly. The leather-clad spectators cheered and yahooed. The referee thought for a moment then gave Eastern Heights a scrum.

Twenty minutes gone. Half-time.

The Welton Wonderers gathered in a gasping, heaving circle. They were five points down.

Chapter 23

The Wonderers gathered together, gulping at the orange juice supplied by Ms Benge. Holly Potroz stuck a fresh piece of gum in her mouth. Nobody felt like asking what she'd done with the other piece.

"Remember my posters," Ms Benge urged. "You people are the only stars that matter today, so keep playing that way. And don't even ask yourselves if I'm right, 'coz I know I am!"

"Tammy, you come off," said Mr O'Neill. "Dallas goes on."

Dallas looked around the circle of faces. "I'm sorry," he said. "I wanted to see my dad. I hung around near the jail all night, till Mum found me this morning. Sorry, guys."

"No worries," chorused ten voices. Then all ten laughed at once, making the Eastern Heights team look across in surprise.

"You're here now," said Silina. "Now we can win the game."

Dallas stared at the ground. "I'd like Ira to be captain for the rest of the game, Mr O'Neill."

Mr O'Neill nodded. As the team trotted back onto the field, he urged "Back up! Back up!"

The referee blew her whistle, and the second half of the championship final began. After just two minutes, Welton were suddenly, shockingly, seven points further behind.

The Wonderers were given a penalty just inside the Eastern Heights half. They went straight into a huddle. Holly slipped the ball up her jersey while the others pretended to do the same. They broke in all directions, yelling and sprinting, and Holly began her run to the goal line.

Five Eastern Heights boys were waiting for her. Holly was tagged from all sides at once. She let the ball go, as she had to; Eastern Heights snatched it up and set off downfield in a bunch. Dean tagged one, Kenny tagged another, but there were too many of them. 7-17. The conversion wobbled over. 7-19. The Welton supporters were hushed.

"They know our moves!" Shayne wheezed as the Wonderers prepared to kick off again. "They must have asked the other teams. They know our moves!"

It was then that Ira took over. "Back up!" he roared as Eastern Heights attacked once more.

142

Ani rushed to help Holly while two boys ran at her. Both boys were tagged.

"Silina! Murdoch! Touchline!" Ira yelled to his team's fastest runners, who were starting to drift infield. Murdoch tore back to the sideline, just in time to block Troy McCracken trying to make a break.

"Here, Dean! Here!" bellowed Ira, as the figure in contact lenses looked for someone to pass to. Ira took the ball and thundered nearly forty metres before Eastern Heights got to him.

The Welton Wonderers' captain was running and passing and backing up like two people. So was Ani, who, with Tammy off the field, seemed determined to play for both of them.

With ten minutes to go it was Ani who grabbed the ball that the Eastern Heights softball smasher had to drop when Dallas appeared out of nowhere and tagged him. Ani scooped it off the ground just like in practice. She threw a dummy pass and beat one boy. Then she threw a cut-out pass that skimmed straight past Tu and the boy marking him, and landed in Ira's hands. Ira charged down-field like a startled elephant. As Jay Viliamu came running at him, Ira flicked a perfect pass back to Kenny, who skidded across the line. Murdoch sent the conversion cleanly between the posts. 14-19.

Eight minutes to go. Ira, roaring and rushing,

stampeded through another gap and sent his second long pass of the day curving into Silina's hands. Silina sped for the corner but was tagged by Jay Viliamu just a metre short of the line. The fastest, best-looking boy in the Eastern Heights team flashed Silina a brilliant smile. She was still concentrating too hard to notice.

Five minutes to go. Eastern Heights attacked. Troy McCracken sidestepped through a gap and was suddenly in the clear. Shayne, muttering "Three metres ... ten metres ... right angle," was in the right place just as suddenly, and tagged him.

Three minutes to go. The Welton parents and brothers and sisters and friends were screaming their heads off. The Welton players were gasping, calling to one another, trying everything they could. Still 14-19.

Two minutes to go. Holly hooked the ball beautifully from a scrum. Ira ran left, dodged right, and aimed a pass at Murdoch. A desperate Eastern Heights defender pushed Murdoch before the ball reached him. The referee's whistle shrilled. Penalty to Welton Intermediate.

One minute to go.

"Scorpio!" growled Ira to his team.

"But they know —" Dean began.

"They know our moves," Kenny finished.

"Just do it!" Ira glared. "Scorpio!"

The Welton Wonderers formed a line, all bent over and waiting for the ball. Only Dallas stood off to one side.

Ira tapped the ball with his foot, pretended to pass to the waiting line, then spun towards Dallas, just like in practice. Eastern Heights, crouched waiting, recognised the move. They rushed at the lone figure.

But Ira didn't pass to Dallas. He didn't pass to anyone. He held onto the ball himself and shot towards the goal line. "Back up!" he yelled. "Back up!"

Without even thinking about it, the Wonderers did so. Murdoch was suddenly beside Ira for a pass. Then Tu, calling "Here! Here!"

As Eastern Heights scrambled across, Tu flicked the ball to Dean. To Holly. To Silina. Back inside to Ani. Back to Ira again.

Ira rose on his toes and threw his third giant pass of the game. Back across the field it spiralled, to where Dallas still stood, all by himself. Dallas swept forward, dodged Jay Viliamu, swerved inside Troy McCracken, stumbled, straightened, and collapsed over the goal line. 19-19.

Murdoch placed the ball for the conversion. There was total silence in the crowd. Half the Wonderers couldn't bear to look. The other half were praying under their breath. Murdoch stepped forward and kicked the ball cleanly over the bar and between the posts.

The referee blew a long blast on her whistle. "Full-time!"

Full-time. Welton Intermediate Wonderers 21; Eastern Heights Intermediate 19.

The crowd exploded.

It was ten minutes before the Wonderers could leave Top Field to get changed. Parents and kids pounded their backs. Mr O'Neill and Ms Benge hugged them, then hugged each other while everyone clapped and whistled. A crowd of Welton supporters lifted Murdoch and Dallas and Ira on their shoulders and carried them around the field. Even the Eastern Heights players came over and shook the Wonderers' hands.

Silina suddenly noticed what good-looking guys Troy and Jay were.

"Great game!" everyone was saying. "Great game!"

The referee shook everyone's hand, too. Parents took photos, and Murdoch looked panic-stricken when he realised he didn't have a comb on him.

Dallas was talking to Silina when the team finally escaped into the quiet of the school corridor.

". . . going to see him next weekend," Kenny

heard Dallas say. "Would you like … sometime…?"

Silina nodded.

Hell, thought Kenny, it's these quiet ones you've got to watch, all right. But he didn't mind. He didn't mind anything after a game like that.

He didn't mind that Murdoch had a new T-shirt saying MR PERFECT. He didn't mind that as they came down from Top Field, a small, spiky-haired figure had appeared beside him.

"Whayugga—" Holly paused and swallowed. "What you gonna play for *summer* sports, Kenny?"

The last of the Welton Wonderers to reach the corridor was Shayne. He looked worried.

"Hey, listen everyone! Eastern Heights say they know exactly how to beat us next time. They've got this secret plan!"

"What … are they gonna give everyone in their team a calculator?" Tu grinned.

"Get real!" Shayne replied. "Nah, they reckon next time they play us they're gonna put four girls in their team, too. That way they'll waste us for sure…"

ⱵIPPO GHOST

Summer Visitors
Emma thinks she's in for a really boring summer,
until she meets the Carstairs family on the beach.
But there's something very *strange* about her
new friends. . .
Carol Barton

Ghostly Music
Beth loves her piano lessons. So why have they
started to make her *ill*. . . ?
Richard Brown

A Patchwork of Ghosts
Who is the evil-looking ghost tormenting Lizzie,
and why does he want to hurt her...?
Angela Bull

The Ghosts who Waited
Everything's changed since Rosy and her family
moved house. Why has everyone suddenly
turned against her. . .?
Dennis Hamley

The Railway Phantoms
Rachel has visions. She dreams of two children
in strange, disintegrating clothes. And it seems
as if they are trying to contact her...
Dennis Hamley

The Haunting of Gull Cottage

Unless Kezzie and James can find what really happened in Gull Cottage that terrible night many years ago, the haunting may never stop...

Tessa Krailing

The Hidden Tomb

Can Kate unlock the mystery of the curse on Middleton Hall, before it destroys the Mason family...?

Jenny Oldfield

The House at the End of Ferry Road

The house at the end of Ferry Road has just been built. So it can't be haunted, can it...?

Martin Oliver

Beware! This House is Haunted
This House is Haunted Too!

Jessica doesn't believe in ghosts. So who *is* writing the strange, spooky messages?

Lance Salway

The Children Next Door

Laura longs to make friends with the children next door. But they're not quite what they seem...

Jean Ure

HIPPO ANIMAL

Have you ever longed for a puppy to love, or a horse of your own? Have you ever wondered what it would be like to make friends with a wild animal? If so, then you're sure to fall in love with these fantastic titles from Hippo Animal!

Thunderfoot
Deborah van der Beek
When Mel finds the enormous, neglected horse Thunderfoot, she doesn't know it will change her life for ever…

Vanilla Fudge
Deborah van der Beek
When Lizzie and Hannah fall in love with the same dog, neither of them will give up without a fight…

A Foxcub Named Freedom
Brenda Jobling
An injured vixen nudges her young son away from her. She can sense danger and cares nothing for herself – only for her son's freedom…

Goose on the Run

Brenda Jobling

It's an unusual pet – an injured Canada goose.
But soon Josh can't imagine being without him.
And the goose won't let *anyone* take him away
from Josh. . .

Pirate the Seal

Brenda Jobling

Ryan's always been lonely – but then he meets
Pirate and at last he has a real friend...

Animal Rescue

Bette Paul

Can Tessa help save the badgers of Delves Wood
from destruction?

Take Six Puppies

Bette Paul

Anna knows she shouldn't get attached to the
six new puppies at the Millington Farm Dog
Sanctuary, but surely it can't hurt to get just a
little bit fond of them...

Goosebumps

R.L. Stine

Reader beware, you're in for a scare!

These terrifying tales will send shivers up your spine:

Goosebumps

Give Yourself Goosebumps

A scary new series from R.L. Stine – where
you decide what happens!

Choose from over 20 scary endings!

Goosebumps

Reader beware – here's THREE TIMES the scare!

Look out for these bumper GOOSEBUMPS editions. With three spine-tingling stories by R.L. Stine in each book, get ready for three times the thrill … three times the scare … three times the GOOSEBUMPS!